WHITE NOISE IS HEAVENLY BLUE

Book One of The Jenny Trilogy

Tabbie Browne

First published Sept 2009.

ISBN: 978-1-291-98196-4

PublishNation, London
www.publishnation.co.uk

This book is dedicated to:

My Father, Ronald, for his inspiration.

My husband, Roy, who realised what I was doing whilst he was fishing.

My sister, Kath, the other half of my brain, with opposite views.

My Dear Friend Pearl, who, for a decade never gave up hope that this novel would reach the outside world.

Other titles by this author

The Spiral (Book Two of The Jenny Trilogy)
The Unforgivable Error
No – Don't!

COMING SOON
Choler (Book Three of The Jenny Trilogy)

Visit the author's website at:
www.tabbiebrowneauthor.com

Chapter 1

Jenny lay back on the lounger and closed her eyes. The remains of the late afternoon sun filtered through the trees and flickered across her relaxed form. It had been a good summer and the earth still held the warmth it had soaked as if storing for colder days to come.

The setting was peaceful. A young woman in her early twenties with seemingly not a care in the world, relaxing as if nothing mattered. Her mother viewed the scene from the kitchen window and a little frown appeared.

"What will become of her?" She almost whispered the question to herself as she sighed with motherly love. The pain of worry was etched on her face. She gave herself a little shake, forced a smile and called through the open window "Fancy a cold drink love?". She was not surprised at the silence which followed.

"Jenny".

A slight stirring from her daughter. "Hmm?"

"Would you like a cold drink?"

"Oh, no I'm OK. Thanks Mum".

"Well you need one Kate" she told herself firmly and making a glass of iced lemon she sat at the table and pondered.

Her little cottage in the heart of Oxfordshire was an idyllic place, the sort most people dream of buying when they retire. Quiet, secluded, quite perfect. Kate had lived here all her life and when she married a lad from a nearby village, he moved in. Her parents had always liked young Jimmy, as they called him and as her father had died just before her wedding it suited them and her mother for them all to stay together. After her mother's death the place became theirs. Kate, not being very nomadic was content to stay where her roots were. Jimmy idolised her and when Jenny was born their happiness seemed complete.

Their daughter attended the village school, was quite bright but always preferred her own company to that of other children. In fact she liked to be on her own most of the time. The teacher had become quite concerned on more than one occasion and visited Kate and Jimmy to try to bottom the problem.

"It's not natural" she would say " a child of that age should be surrounded by others of her class. But does she? No. She won't have them near her." Whilst the parents appreciated what she was saying they often wondered if she actually aggravated the situation by pushing Jenny into something she didn't want. When they approached her themselves she merely clammed up. She wasn't rude. She just wanted to be by herself.

Kate sat musing over the childhood days casting the odd glance to where Jenny lay. Again her mind was drawn back as if she was forced to retrace the girl's life to undergo some form of mental torment.

It was no better when she went to Burford. They had both hoped the change of school at the age of eleven might trigger a feeling of camaraderie when she met new people. If anything, Jenny was treated as something a bit different. She still didn't mix. Did her lessons, played games got through all her exams with good marks. But didn't make friends. At the parent-teacher evenings the story was the same. "I'm sorry Mr. and Mrs. Hedges, but Jenny doesn't seem to need anyone else in her life". Some would try the path of "We must do something about it, she can't go through life like that you know". Eventually they all gave up with the attitude "If she won't be helped, well---".

Jenny could never understand what all the fuss was about. If other children wanted to play together, fine. She didn't try to interfere with them, so why couldn't she be left alone. And of course, there were her 'colours'. None of the other children ever spoke about having 'colours' so perhaps they didn't see them as she did. An instinct had always guided her not to speak of things which were hers. Things about which others would not understand. When people don't understand things they ridicule. Ever since she could remember, this was an inborn understanding.

She had always been able to close her eyes and watch her 'colours'. Unspeakable shades that merged and floated. Nothing she had ever seen with her eyes open could compare with the hues that passed before her closed lids. Starting as an irregular circle with the strange depth of bottomless colour in the centre, the image would glide to a corner to be followed immediately by another forming. She had tried to hang on to one to save it from disappearing but all in vain. "Bubbles" she thought at the time. "They are like bubbles". But no, bubbles were light and transparent and these -- these were almost like looking into a deep hole, or into space, beautifully coloured space.

There was never any need to share her knowledge. Why try to explain what others could not see. It wasn't as if she could show anyone.

It was just after her fourteenth birthday she heard it. Faintly at first. Hardly there at all. Gradually over the months it got steadily louder and always happened at the same time, just as she went to bed. Then she realised that each day it was lasting longer. Not much at first, probably a few seconds but it was all building into a regular occurrence.

To begin with it was little more than then the whisper of a gentle breeze when the air is just being stirred. Then it became more of a rustling turning into a crackle. Her child's mind could only identify with sounds she already knew, so it was some years later when she realised that what she had experienced was the noise static makes.
Again, this was not something to discuss. With anyone.

On leaving school at sixteen, Jenny got a job at an estate agents in Chipping Norton. She soon settled in, was well liked and got on with her work in her normal quiet manner which suited her boss. Her immediate superior was a mature woman, Mrs. Randle who kept her eye closely on Jenny but didn't crowd her. She realised this girl was different from your run of the mill school leavers. This one was deep.

When she felt she had gained enough of Jenny's confidence, she started talking to her during lunch breaks. Nothing fancy, just idle little bits of news. Then one day she ventured "I hope it doesn't bother you, but I am a medium." Mrs. Randle sat back to watch the reaction. Jenny stared her straight in the face and replied

"Why should it bother me?. If you are happy with it".

"Well you're a right one to be sure". Mrs. R. had expected more surprise. "Aren't you even a little curious?"

Jenny thought for a moment. "I've never given it much thought". then "Do you see things?"

Mrs. Randle brightened "I knew you had it in you".

Jenny was on the defensive as if her private little world was about to be invaded. The older woman continued.

"You're a bright one you are. I bet you've had experiences".

There was no way Jenny was going to be drawn this easily, so getting up and collecting up the remains of her lunch she said "I'm not into that sort of thing, sorry".

Mrs. Randle sat back satisfied. "That will do for now," she thought" I've planted the seed".

If Jenny was into anything, it was medical dictionaries. The noise in her head must have a cause. She wasn't bothered about the 'colours' because they had always been there, but this noise was getting worse. And it wasn't only at night, it was any time when she could switch off and be quiet. To tune in as she put it. There was no way she would entertain the idea of going to a doctor about it, so she poured over pages of complaints which could afford a logical explanation. To no avail. If she found a description remotely resembling her problem, it never quite matched and she would start looking all over again.

Mrs. Randle had been very patient awaiting a golden opportunity to pounce. One day she and Jenny were having their lunch and casually she ventured "When you are going to have a vision, you see a bright blue flash of light first. Did you know that?"

Jenny was caught off guard. "Blue?" But she quickly composed herself feeling very vulnerable for some reason.

"I thought you might find that interesting". Mrs. Randle sat back with a self satisfied look on her face.

Jenny was back to her normal self. "Like I said before, I don't bother with that sort of thing".

"Of course you don't, I'm just telling you things you may be interested in. You see, I can't tell everyone, but I thought you might understand".

"Me, why me?" Jenny felt uncomfortable, even threatened.

"Oh nothing sinister dear, you seem a very caring sort of person. You wouldn't laugh". This woman knew just what she was doing.

Jenny relaxed a little. "Oh no, I wouldn't laugh".

"It's lonely you see". Mrs. Randle looked into space as if speaking to herself.

The girl eyed her carefully before replying. "You mean because you don't like to tell anyone?"

There was a moment's pause, carefully timed, before the older woman slowly turned to face her newly found audience.

"You have to be careful, I mean people are afraid of what they don't understand. Don't you agree Jenny?"

Caution jumped to the foreground of the girl's mind.

"I'm sure you know what you are talking about".

This reply wasn't as forthcoming as the questioner had hoped and Mrs. Randle knew she would have some task getting the girl to open up. But she knew there was something different about this one, whatever it was.

Jenny was aware she was being probed but she paid little heed as it seemed unimportant. What was important was the merging of her colours with her noise. She hadn't realised it was happening, until one evening when she was watching television on her own, the ringing in her ears started to drown the music. Without thinking, she closed her eyes for a second and the colours, more vivid than ever vibrated in time to the noise. As if governed by an unseen force she was unable to open her eyes for what felt like minutes. When she could, the ringing stopped abruptly.

She sat for a moment pondering. There was something a little unnerving about this. For someone who had always felt alone, she was no longer alone. But what was most unsettling was she didn't feel in control, instead she felt as though she was being manipulated in some way.

"It's her" she said to herself, thinking Mrs. Randle had something to do with this. But logic soon dispelled that. The colours had been there ever since she could remember. The noises had been there since grammar school. All before she met the medium, or whatever she called herself. So it must be something else. But there was one thing Jenny felt sure about now, the noise did not have a medical cause. Whatever was producing it would not be found in a dictionary.

Kate and Jimmy had no other children, not by choice, it just happened that way. They had always felt blessed at having been given a normal healthy child and it didn't matter which sex it was as long as it was alright. They shared concern over Jenny's self-contained manner but decided that, if that was the way she was, they couldn't change it. As long as she was happy. and she seemed to be, in her own way.

They were both relieved when she settled into her job and they relaxed into feeling that life would run smoothly from then on. Little did they expect the events which lay before them.

Jenny quite liked Mrs. Randle. The woman helped and advised her with her work and seemed friendly enough, but the old wariness was never far from the surface. The odd spiritual sentences crept into the conversation but the medium was careful not to let Jenny feel trapped or cornered and changed the subject when she felt the barriers go up. However, sometimes they would have almost in depth discussions.

"You build with thought bricks you see." Mrs Randle was explaining how she got all the things she wanted.

"I don't want for much, I mean I don't want many things." Jenny didn't want to give the wrong impression.

"No, I gathered that. But there's always something, it doesn't have to be a big thing."

Trying to get the emphasis away from herself, Jenny asked "What are you building for now then?"

"A car."

"A car?" Jenny couldn't hide her surprise. "That's not exactly small. Will you get it do you think?"

"Oh yes."

"You seem very sure. What if it doesn't work?"

Mrs. Randle beamed. "Oh it will work, it always does." She continued "It's positive thinking. If you believe you can get something, or do something, you will".

"So," Jenny paused, "This is all through you being a medium is it?"

"Anyone can think positively. But my experiences, my visions taught me to do it." Mrs. Randle knew she had Jenny's interest now.

"What kind of visions?" She almost hated herself for asking.

"I have them for other people mostly."

"In what way?" Jenny was curious, but was still directing the conversation away from herself. Even now she was not prepared to divulge her secret feelings.

"Well, people ask me to go to their houses or a special place, and I pick up vibrations. Sometimes they want to hear from a loved one who has passed over. You know."

"Do you, um, -----"

"Yes?" Mrs. R. wasn't going to let this go.

"You said something about colours, blue wasn't it?"

"Oh blue, yes. Very important colour. God's colour. Why do you ask?"

This was not what Jenny wanted. She was not going to get caught in this little trap.

"Oh nothing really, it's just interesting the way you talk. I don't know anything about it."

"But you have experiences?"

"No, no nothing like that."

As far as Jenny was concerned that was the end of the conversation. She had found out nothing new from this person who thought she had felt something unusual. Well maybe she had. But that wasn't her business.

"These people" she thought "think they know it all, but they know nothing." She had half expected Mrs. Randle to describe the colours and noise but it was quite obvious she had never encountered anything so spectacular, or she would have been forced to brag about it.

But one lesson was learned from this relationship. Jenny was even more certain than ever that she was special, she musn't tell anyone and above all, she was not alone.

Chapter 2

Kate finished her drink and glanced at the kitchen clock. "Better start the evening meal" she thought reluctantly. Recent events had taken the wind out of her sails and she had little enthusiasm for the daily chores. Again she glanced towards her daughter's relaxed body and again was forced to reflect on the milestones which had left the scars, not only on the young person stretched out under the trees but on Jimmy and most of all, on her.

Her mind switched instantly to Jenny's eighteenth birthday. Nothing dramatic had been planned as that's how the teenager wanted it.

"What friends do I have?" she had asked her mother. "I don't need a party."

"But it's your eighteenth, that's special." Kate had almost pleaded with her but refusing to give up said "Well let's just have Auntie Doris round, and what about your work people?"

Jenny grimaced. "Mum."

"Alright, alright. But it doesn't seem right, not to do anything I mean." Kate was quite disappointed. Any mother looks forward to special days in her child's life and this was one of them. Only it wouldn't be.

"I um -- " Jenny started as if to say something that was difficult to voice.

"I did think of going to Oxford, to the theatre or something."

Kate eyed her suspiciously. "On your own? You never go out on your own, well only for walks, I mean you don't go places and certainly not the theatre."

Jenny turned away. "You've always said I should."

"I know dear, but on your birthday."

Jenny thought for a moment. "Well, maybe not exactly on the day, I'm not sure. Have the family to tea if you like." She felt she had to make some effort to make amends for the disappointment her mother could not hide.

This was going to have to do. Kate knew from experience just how much rope could be stretched and she was at full stretch. But one thing was niggling at her. Why this sudden interest in the outside world. Of course she welcomed it but she felt sure she was not getting the whole story. But the girl would tell her in her own time.

The truth was that Jenny had met a young man. He had been visiting her place of work and, very casually started talking to her. When he asked her to go out with him she refused automatically. But something about him seemed different to anyone else she knew. He had a special magnetism, a charisma and she found herself regretting her impulse to protect her world. So when he asked her the second time she agreed to go.

His name was Matthew Gavrielle. His blond hair and deep set blue eyes were enough to make any young heart flutter. A guess at his age would hover around 24 - 26 but his knowledge defied this for there seemed to be no subject on earth on which he could not converse. Jenny found this fascinating. For once in her life she had met someone with whom she could hold an in depth conversation and not have to force small talk which led nowhere. Their first date proved this. Instead of suggesting a visit to the pictures, which was the usual ritual, Matthew asked Jenny if she would like to go for a walk. Normally a girl approaching eighteen would be a little wary but this seemed the most natural thing, almost as if this was a pattern in her life and she must follow it.

"I will call for you on Saturday" this was not a request, it was a definite statement.

Jenny nodded in agreement. "But you don't know where I live, I haven't told you yet."

"Then I suggest you remedy that immediately."

As she explained the whereabouts of her little home just outside Shipton, she had the strangest feeling that this was merely a formality and he already knew more about her than he had divulged.

"Till Saturday." Matthew gave Jenny a swift smile and was gone.

"The day before my birthday," she mused,"the best present I could have."

On returning home that evening, Jenny made a point of talking to her mother before her father came in.

"So it's all settled for Sunday for my birthday tea?"

Kate welcomed this bit of enthusiasm. "Yes dear, Aunt Doris has got your cousin Anne staying so they are both coming. Are you sure there is no-one else?"

"No really Mum, that will be just fine." She paused for a moment then said "I'm going out on Saturday, by the way, just thought I'd let you know."

Kate brightened. "Oh that's nice, who with?"

"Oh nobody special, just someone who comes into work occasionally." Jenny tried to make it sound as uninteresting as possible. But her Mother was naturally curious.

"Man?"

"Well, yes it is actually, we're just going for a walk that's all."

Kate wanted to know more. "Well, why not ask him to tea as well, on your birthday?"

"Oh no Mum, I hardly know him, he might find it pushy." Feeling herself being edged into a corner she left the room with a flounce saying "I'm going to freshen up before dinner". End of conversation.

As her mother busied about preparing the meal she said aloud "She's going out with a man, and he's taking her for a WALK? Isn't that just typical?"

Matthew approached the rose covered porch and was about to knock the door when it opened.

"I saw you coming." Jenny's face held expectancy. "I'm ready".

Kate appeared immediately behind her, instantly approving of this handsome fellow who now stood beaming at them both.

"Well, ladies, do I have a choice? Which of you is it to be?"

"Oh really," Kate faked coyness but added "Jenny where are your manners, why don't you introduce your friend?"

"Oh sorry Mum. This is Matthew, we're going for a walk."

Matthew extended his hand and gave Kate's a firm shake. "Don't worry Mrs. Hedges, I'll take good care of her."

"I've no doubt about that, Matthew You don't hear that name much, biblical isn't it?"

"It goes back a long way." He held out his arm and Jenny linked hers into it so naturally as if he had always been there.

"Do come in for a cup of tea when you get back". Kate wasn't going to let him go any sooner than she could.

"Very kind, thank you." His smile melted Kate until her knees trembled, not visibly she hoped.

"Bye Mum" Jenny went off with a spring in her step never before seen.

The mother watched them go thinking "I'd have more than a spring in my step if that were me."

"I thought we'd head off towards South Lawn, if that's OK?" Matthew had a way of asking although it was clear he had already decided the matter in hand.

"Fine by me, I like that road". Jenny wouldn't have minded where they went, she had a feeling this day would be special.

As they set off at a casual pace Jenny turned to her escort with a puzzled look. "I'm surprised you know such a small place, it's only a few houses apart from the big house itself. I wouldn't expect everyone to know about it."

"Never confuse me with 'everyone." Matthew gave a friendly smile which signalled "Ask no more".

The road led out of Shipton towards Burford. There was a more direct route but that was the main road and was not in keeping with this outing.

"The school bus always used to get stuck coming up here." Jenny felt she was being informative. "We used to love it, the snow came right up the front of the bus, it was so deep."

"Because of the drifting." The explanation was finished for her.

"Why, yes, you sound as if you'd seen it." She gave him a curious glance.

"I can imagine." Was all he would offer.

After climbing steadily they had reached a point where the view reached for miles. The man turned the girl round slowly until they were overlooking the village. He led her to a low wall and they both sat listening to the sounds of nature. The quietness almost echoed as it travelled on the slight breeze just stirring the grasses and roadside plants. The birdsong touched them as the winged creatures passed. All felt peaceful in the world.

Without realising, Jenny had closed her eyes and immediately her 'colours' were floating in time to the singing in her head. But there was more. The colours were forming into recognisable shapes, flowers then flower beds, then whole gardens of never ending colour. The static had become meaningful, angelic, almost like a choral accompaniment to the visions. She travelled on air through this world of wonderment as though she had no body and she was existing in her mind only, witnessing new brilliant arrays of living colour and hearing heavenly strains so sweet they were indescribable.

Other images came and went as though visiting, faces, shapes she could not recognise and she began to feel a little vulnerable. She was aware of a strong arm around her shoulder guiding her back and as she slowly opened her eyes she looked straight into Matthew's. She blinked

"Did I fall asleep? Oh I'm sorry, but was I dreaming?"

Matthew smiled. "No, you didn't fall asleep." Then after a moment "Did you enjoy your trip?"

Jenny's eyes were wide open now. "Wh--What--" She was taken aback and couldn't find the words she was looking for.

"How do I know?" He smiled softly letting his gaze rest on the panorama before them.

"There's a lot you won't understand yet, and I don't want to confuse you." He took her hand but she quickly drew it away.

"What do you mean? Understand what?" She was uneasy. Her world was being penetrated and she wasn't sure if she liked it. Everything had been alright when she had kept her images to herself and she had felt exhilarated at the new experience, but the bit that was causing unrest was the fact that it was no longer hers alone. Not if somebody else knew about it, and she felt this man knew a lot more than she would be happy with.

"Don't be so defensive, it's often a shock at first." He took her hand back in his. "Let me tell you a little for now, you may feel more comfortable."

"What do you mean, 'at first'?" Jenny was disappointed. Today was not a bit what she had expected.

"You have always thought you could see and hear things that other people couldn't." Matthew waited for her acknowledgment before continuing.

"You mean, other people get them too?" She didn't know whether to be relieved or upset. "I'm not like that medium I work with?"

"Not exactly."

"So what am I?" She was on the verge of tears.

"I'll tell you what you are. You're special." Again he waited.

Jenny brightened a little. "I suppose I've always known there was something, I just didn't expect anyone to know or explain it to me. Anyway, how do you know so much?"

"Ah, I wondered when you would get to that." He sat back and studied her for a minute. "Am I not familiar?"

Jenny looked closely. "You are, but I don't know why. I feel as if I have known you for longer than I really have."

"Then my dear girl you haven't been studying your images have you?"

"Your face! It's your face that's been appearing isn't it?" She was beaming now. "I knew I wasn't alone, was it you? How long have you been with me? Why did you leave it till now to ----?"

Matthew held up his hand. "One question at a time, but first tell me, do you feel a little more comfortable?"

"Oh yes, thanks, but tell me more." There was no holding her now. She wasn't frightened and was burning for an explanation of the experience she had just encountered.

"Don't be alarmed." Matthew began," Yes I've been with you ever since you were born but only recently shown you my face in an image. I thought you would recognise me, that was the reason for it."

"Like a premonition?"

"It goes a lot deeper, but understand it that way for now if you find it easier. It's a start."

Chapter 3

Kate's mind slipped back to the present for a moment. "That's when it all started, on her eighteenth birthday" the words came out with a rush. She had rearranged the facts so many times in her head to make sense of everything. She loved Jimmy dearly, but he wouldn't understand, she had tried many times to discuss it with him but he either didn't think anything was the matter, or he didn't want to. "We just want a quiet life dear," he would say.

"Well, I want a quiet life too, but how can I?" Her gaze again settled on Jenny's calm form. So different from the rages she endured in her sleep.

"If only I knew, if only she could confide in me." Kate's hands went to her head in despair. "I could help her if I knew what I was up against".

Again she drifted to the day before the girl's eighteenth birthday. "She was different from then on, she changed." Kate could still recall the sight of the two walking off arm in arm, as though that was when her little girl walked out of her life and a stranger returned.

Still sitting on the low wall with Matthew's arm around her shoulder, Jenny was under his spell. "When you say 'a start', does that mean there is a lot more?"

"More than you can ever imagine, but you must trust me. For I can only reveal a little at a time."

"Why?" Jenny wanted to know it all now.

"Because my little elfin, it is too vast for you to absorb. You will see. Be patient." His look defied her to argue.

"O.K. But explain how you have been with me all my life."

"That" he paused "is an excellent place to begin and I would have been disappointed in you had you not asked that."

"You see, that's what I mean" Jenny was astounded "you expect things of me that I'm not ready for. And another thing?"

"Yes?"

"Have you been watching everything I've ever done?" She frowned a little.

"Not at all." Matthew gave a small laugh. "Think of it as being on the end of a telephone."

"Go on," she was determined not to interrupt again.

"If I phoned you, we could talk"

She nodded.

"Then when we hung up, you wouldn't know what I was doing, nor I you. Right?"

"Ye-es" she thought she was with him so far.

"Then, when we wanted to communicate again, one of us would ring the other". He sat back giving her time to digest this.

"Only you didn't phone, of course---" she looked at him for reassurance.

He nodded slowly, "No, go on, what did I do?"

"You were in my colours" she was excited, "you came into my visions. It was when the sounds merged, wasn't it, wasn't it?" Jenny had never been so elated in her whole life. Perhaps there was a meaning to it all, and perhaps it wasn't so bad sharing it especially when someone could explain it.

"Call it the ringing tone" he joked and they both laughed.

"But of course" he was serious again "I don't only use sound waves." He paused again, "light waves too, but that's nothing new."

"Now you are loosing me." Jenny said but hastened to add" but go on, I will understand won't I?"

"You will, in time, but your brain cannot cope with the full extent of what you will see, and learn, unless I feed it to you slowly. Promise me you will pace yourself."

He stood up and helped Jenny to her feet. "Time to be going my little elfin, I could drink that cup of tea now."

"Oh Matthew, you don't know how good I feel."

His face clouded. "A word of warning. You will see pleasant things, but if you should see an image repulsive to you, open your eyes immediately and put it from your mind."

Jenny was a little worried. She had enjoyed the 'garden' trip so much and had never seen anything that wasn't nice, so what did he mean?

As if reading her thoughts he merely said "Where there is good there is also bad. It's the balance of things."

Taking her hand, they walked leisurely down the hill back to the cottage where Kate greeted them warmly with tea and home made cakes. They spent a relaxed time talking together, and much as the mother tried, she found out little about this handsome young man who was to become an integral part of Jenny's life.

Also she could not resist the opportunity of inviting him to Jenny's birthday tea the following day.

"Mother, I'm sure Matthew has other plans already." There was no way he was going to be subjected to scrutiny, because that's what would happen.

But the problem was solved for her.

"I'm very sorry," he apologised "but I am seeing my parents tomorrow, or I would have loved to have accepted."

"No you wouldn't" thought Jenny "you don't want a crowd any more than I do. We aren't like that". She mused for a moment. How easily she had used the word 'we'.

"Jenny." Her mother's voice made her jump."Are you dreaming?"

"What, oh- no -sorry Mum."

"Matthew's going now but I've made him promise to come again soon. Are you going to see him to the door dear?"

"Oh yes."

Kate made herself scarce while the two left the cottage and walked to the gate.

“That’s a very unusual surname you have." Jenny looked enquiringly into his face."

"What? Gavrielle? Yes I don't suppose you hear it much."

"It's a bit like Gabriel. I shall call you my archangel Gabriel." She gave a satisfied little nod. "Yes, I like that."

"Oh dear, I should have changed my name.” He held her face in his hands, kissed her lightly on the lips and whispered "I'll see you on Tuesday for your next lesson, little elfin. You will be free won't you?" Again this was not a request but a definite statement.

"Of course." she whispered. Within seconds he had gone and she slowly made her way to the kitchen to help her mother.

Kate smiled "What a nice young man dear, will you see him again?" There was a slight pause before the reply. "Tuesday".

"Oh, that's nice. Where are you going this time?"

Jenny thought "Do you know, he didn't say, perhaps the same".

"Oh". Kate's face fell. She had hoped it would be something a little more interesting than just a walk.

The birthday tea was tolerable. Jenny sat through most of it without saying much.

"She's still quiet, isn't she. Thought she might have grown out of it by now." Aunt Doris tried to whisper without much success.

"Oh she's alright" Kate was quick to cover any attack on her daughter, "She's doing very well at work, aren't you dear?" and without waiting for a reply turned back to her sister and said "We can't all be the same, can we?"

"Thanks Mum" thought Jenny. She had surfaced for a moment but had spent most of the meal deep in her own self.

Jimmy reached for a piece of home made bread "Ah, she's no trouble are you lass?" Jenny shook her head.

"How are you doing these days Anne?" Kate tried to move the attention to her niece, "We don't see much of you now do we?"

"Ah well, she's always very busy, aren't you Anne? She's a student nurse in Cheltenham, doesn't get much time to come and see us. We're very proud of her."

The two young ladies exchanged glances which led into a smirk. There was no need for them to offer anything by the way of conversation, the mothers would do it for them.

After a polite elapse of time the visitors took their leave with promises of "We must do this more often", which everyone knew would never happen.

Jimmy settled back in his armchair and reached for the newspaper. Smiling at his daughter he said "I'm proud of you, never mind the likes o' them."

"Thanks Dad, you're the best." and Jenny gave him a loving pat as she passed his chair.

Jenny decided to have an early night. There had been too many people for her liking and she wanted to 'tune in'. Last night had been nothing spectacular, but after the afternoon session she couldn't really complain. She lay on her bed looking up at the sky through the window. Her curtains were never drawn as she had always been attracted by the stars twinkling in the night, and wondering who was out there, far away.

As her eyes closed, the colours were there instantly together with the crackling almost whistling high pitched noise.

"I wonder if I can only travel with him." The thought raced across her brain. "Well we shall see." Logic took over as she recalled his words of warning. "Of course I can travel alone or he wouldn't have told me to beware of bad things."

She closed her eyes and totally relaxed until her body seemed to be floating. It was a pleasant sensation at first until she felt she was floating over a dark bottomless hole. Panic entered her world. It did not occur to her to open her eyes or stop her relaxed state. Instead she continued to float until she was lifted at speed high up and away as if being rescued from the darkness.

She began to see faces floating before her. Not live ones, statues, masks, fixed expressions. The noise became almost piercing as the light changed to blinding white, flashing past her as though she was being propelled through it. She wanted to scream "What's happening" but she could not. Although her mouth was open wide, no sound came out.

Suddenly, she came to earth with a bang. As she opened her eyes she saw her mother bending over her.

"Jenny, Jenny, what's the matter?"

As her senses returned Jenny looked round the room and realised she had been no-where. No black pit, no faces.

"Sorry Mum, I must have been dreaming." then as an afterthought "Why are you here?"

"You were shouting, no screaming more like. It must have been a nightmare."

"Oh sorry, had you gone to bed" she realised her mother was in her nighty.

Jimmy appeared in the doorway.

"Is she alright?"

"Yes I'm alright Dad. What time is it?"

Her mother looked at the bedside clock. "Half past one."

"What?"

Kate straightened the bedclothes as if tucking up a little child. "Will you be alright now?"

"I'll be fine now thanks, sorry Mum, sorry Dad."

Both parents left her room and closed the door.

"She's never done that before." Kate was thoughtful as they got back into bed.

"Oh probably just a one-off, I shouldn't worry too much" Jimmy tried to reassure her, but he hadn't seen the look on Jenny's face when Kate had reached her. It was one she didn't want to see again.

Chapter 4

Jenny could hardly wait for Tuesday. She wanted to explain her experience to Matthew and see what explanation he would give. What she had felt on her own was nothing like the calm beauty surrounding her when her guardian was there.

"This is all very new" she thought as she travelled home from work on the day of her next date. "It's as though I'm on the brink of a new life. The new me starts here." The words were almost audible she was so elated. Almost. Something brought her back to her senses. There was something about her last vivid experience which left an uneasy feeling in her stomach. Again she did not feel alone, only this time it wasn't pleasant.

At seven o'clock precisely there was a knock on the door. "I'll go," Jenny was already on her feet. Kate smiled. She enjoyed Jenny's happiness but she too was bewildered by the nightmare, if that's what it was.

"Good evening Mrs. Hedges." Matthew stood by her side.

"Oh hello Matthew, please call me Kate".

"Good evening Kate", he gave a short laugh "it's such a lovely evening, I thought maybe we could walk again, is that alright with you Jenny?"

"I thought you'd suggest that, so I've dressed accordingly." Jenny was on her way to the door.

"She'll be safe with me Kate, don't worry about her." Matthew laid a hand softly on the mother's shoulder.

"Oh I don't, not when she's with you."

With a wave of his hand, he disappeared after Jenny leaving Kate alone to her thoughts.

"Are we going to the same place?" They were hardly out of the garden before Jenny eagerly asked the question.

"Is it special?" he said talking her hand firmly in his.

"It is now." She loved the nearness of him, as though this is what she had been searching all her life, and just found it.

"Then so be it."

They walked in silence for a while, and when Jenny started to voice her fears, he put a finger to her lips to silence her. "All in good time my little elfin." He did not speak until they had found their place on the wall overlooking the village.

"Now," he paused "we can communicate."

Jenny stumbled through her words at first, but soon her feelings flooded out until she had related the unpleasant episode.

"So soon." He said almost to himself. Then after a moments thought he turned and looked her full in the face.

"Remember my warning?" His sternness surprised her.

"But I couldn't open my eyes." she said emphatically.

"Which is why you were brought back suddenly. You will learn to do it for yourself."

Jenny shook her head. "This is all a bit much. How will I learn?"

"Why do you think I am here? I will teach you but you must heed what I say."

They both sat in silence for a minute.

"You see," he looked far away, "I can't always be at your side, not every minute, and there are always those who will tease you, torment you."

"How will I know you are there, I don't see you." She needed reassurance very badly at this moment.

"You don't see the wind, but you know it is blowing. You feel it." He was still staring ahead and she began to feel as though he was in his own world with her on the outside.

"We've left you till now. We chose Jimmy and Kate because we felt they would leave you to develop and grow in your own space, which they did. An ideal setting. Not everyone is so fortunate, too many outside pressures you see. "

Jenny did not see.

"Wow, just a minute." There was a need for an explanation. "Explain 'we chose', you're talking about my parents."

"It's not an accident that you are born into a certain body you know. I thought you would have known that."

"Well, I'm sorry to disappoint you, but I didn't." Jenny was adamant.

He studied her. The dawning of an idea spread over her face.

"You mean reincarnation don't you?"

He shrugged. "Call it that if you like. There's more to it though." Then very carefully he said "What I am going to tell you will take some absorbing, but try and stick with me. You don't have to rush to take it all in at once. But you've got to know sometime and it might as well be now."

Jenny shifted until she was comfortable. Little did she know how unprepared she was for what she was about to hear.

Kate was already looking ahead. As she watched the pair walk slowly away up the hill, her mind was racing. What a find pair they make. Maybe if she settled down she wouldn't have another nightmare and why did she have that one. A bit late to start that, didn't it usually happen to girls a bit younger? Anyway, perhaps Jimmy was right and it was only a one off. She let her imagination run on to a wedding. Jenny's wedding. Oh what a beautiful bride, and what a handsome groom. Wouldn't mind him for a son-in-law. Oh no. He'd have to call me Mother. No, she decided, he could still call me Kate, I would insist.

"What am I doing?" she asked herself. "This is only the second meeting and I've got them married off. Stop it Kate. Take hold of yourself." And she picked up some knitting and tried to concentrate on the tricky pattern, although her mind was still elsewhere.

Jenny looked at Matthew, drinking in his good looks, mesmerised by his soft voice which seemed to be lulling her into a beautiful relaxed state.

"Let me start with something you already know." Matthew's hand twirled a long grass growing at his feet.

"You are aware of several different forms of life, they have always been there and you take them for granted, giving them little or no thought."

Jenny's eyes were closed now and she nodded in agreement. After a slight pause she said" You mean animals and birds and the like."

Matthew stroked her hair “The insect world, fishes in fact everything marine, and what is round you now. Nature. The trees grass, flowers even lichens growing on the stones, these are all life forms."

"Like you said" Jenny agreed "they have been there ever since I can remember. The are part of life."

"They ARE life" he corrected her. Taking a deep breath, knowing what was to come would come as a jolt, he continued slowly.

"The search has been on for many years to find life forms in space. and what do we expect these new beings to be like? Monsters? Blobs of jelly?"

Jenny opened her eyes. "You are changing the subject. I thought you were going to describe the visions."

"Be patient." His finger silenced her."You are already making the mistake that has been made on this planet for years. People must put everything into little boxes and label them. Don't do that."

She was silent and a little nervous.

"Do you want me to continue?" his eyes searched her face.

"Yes, I want to know."

As if to reassure he took her hand in both of his. "Space, aliens, religion, reincarnation, ESP, second sight and even astrology are all in the same package, not separate as mankind would have you believe. If only they would shake off the old beliefs and open their minds, the answers to much of what they seek are there before them." He spoke with such a passion and almost a frustration.

"How do you know all this?" Jenny almost whispered, "and how do I know what you are saying is true?"

"Maybe I should explain where I come from, if you feel you are ready." His head inclined awaiting her reply.

"Yes, yes please." Whatever he was going to say, she might as well hear it all now.

Jimmy walked into the cottage and sat down opposite Kate. "Is she out with him?" The question was an innocent enquiry about their daughter. He never pried.

"Yes, they've gone out for a walk again." Kate frowned at her husband. "Doesn't seem natural if you ask me, just walking and talking. I mean she's never talked to us much, and look at all the problems when she was at school. So why can she talk to him so much?"

Jimmy smiled lovingly at his wife. "Don't take it too much to heart. She's happy with him isn't she?"

"Seems to be." Kate nodded as she spoke.

"Well then, couldn't want much else for her. Just so long as she's happy that's all." He picked up the paper but put it on his lap before opening it. "Hope he doesn't disappoint her though. Shouldn't be happy with that."

"You see" Kate was quick to pick up on his wariness. "You are concerned although you never show it."

"No good fussing without cause. Just don't want to see the lass hurt." With that he opened his paper and started to read. Kate turned back to her knitting with a little sigh. "I suppose we shall have to wait and see."

Matthew took a deep breath. "I have roots else where. I originate from another place. Maybe the only way you will understand is to think of me as an alien."

Jenny was forced to laugh. "Don't be silly, you're human like me."

"Yes" he smiled back at her "I have a human body now, and will have again no doubt. Look, I will simplify it as much as possible. "

Jenny really wanted to understand but this was getting a bit way out. However as she was still captivated by his charisma she felt she had to see it through.

"I'll try not to interrupt." She squeezed his hand.

Matthew smiled. "I appreciate it isn't easy, but it will all fall into place. Some people say they never dream. Others dream and remember what they have dreamt, whilst others can travel at will whilst they are asleep. Also, most people have no recollection of any previous life unless hypnotised. But we, my people, have total recall of every life we have lived and the knowledge gained."

"I'm sorry, but I've got to ask" Jenny held up her hand as if in class.

"No, no go on, I'm pleased."

"Well, I was just thinking," Jenny was interested now, "could that be why you have child prodigies, I mean didn't Mozart compose a symphony or something when he was only twelve?"

"You are on the right track." Matthew was relieved at this response."But the important thing is that existence, or life, call it what you will, does not only consist of a body with a short life span. It continues."

"Life after death!" Jenny was exuberant.

"After, before, all the time. The death of a person is only the end of the vehicle they are using at any given time. You still exist until you are given another life to learn more. It's usual to come back to the same planet, Earth in our case to expand the knowledge built up here."

"I think I am beginning to understand." Jenny was very relaxed. "It would be no good spending one life here, then the next on Mars, or wherever, because there would be no continuity".

"That's the general idea, although things have been known to ---- but let's not complicate matters."

Jenny laughed as she said "I must ask something?"

He smiled "Go on."

"Well, what do you really look like? On your own planet?"

He laughed now. "We're back to the ugly monsters already." Then very gently. "This isn't easy to understand. Let me ask you. What do you think your spirit, or soul, the real you that's inside, what does that look like?"

She thought for a moment. "That's a tough one. I don't know."

"There's your answer."

She was puzzled. "But you must look like something."

"You form your own impression, or the impression you are given. There are entities which can create an image and make you see what they want you to see."

"Is that what happens at séances?" Jenny's mind sprang to Mrs. Randle,

"Very much so. There are many kinds of mischievous pranksters who get up to all sorts of things, but don't worry too much about that for now, except, be careful. Don't believe all you see. Keep your own mind strong."

"But when you are between lives, do you go back to your planet? I mean what are you like then?"

"In simple terms we exist without a body, which is why I cannot describe a form to you. Don't forget there are earthbound beings who have not returned to their source and therefore are unable to be reborn."

"Ghosts." Jenny said.

Matthew stood and pulled Jenny to her feet. "I think that is more than enough for today. Digest this knowledge and let it become part of you.

"Will you take me on another journey through the gardens?"

"No need, you can develop that for yourself. However, there is one journey I would like you to share with me, and it's nothing to do with our other selves.

Don't forget I am in a human body with human emotions."

Jenny's stomach did a somersault as he drew her close and embraced her with his strong arms. At first his lips brushed hers, then unleashed a passion she could never have imagined. After a few moments he guided her back down the hill to her home.

"I will see you tomorrow." He kissed her fondly. "Sweet dreams my little elfin."

And he was gone.

Chapter 5

Kate and Jimmy looked up as Jenny entered the cottage. "Have a good time dear?"

"Lovely thanks." she answered still glowing from his closeness to her.

"Pity Matthew didn't pop in." Kate was quizzing again.

"I expect the lad had to get off home." Jimmy was quick to let his daughter off the hook and gave her a knowing wink.

Kate was not satisfied. She didn't know enough yet.

"Where did you say he lives?"

"I don't think I mentioned it, but it's somewhere over Charlbury way I think." Jenny turned to leave the room.

"Well, he certainly doesn't walk here then. I've never seen a car." She waited for a reply and again Jimmy stepped in.

"Oh he's probably got his own helicopter, leave the lass alone."

"More like his own set of wings" thought Jenny as she went up the winding stairs to her room. As she settled into bed, she closed her eyes and whispered "Good night my archangel Gabriel."

The room still held the warmth of the day and Jenny, contented in her newly found emotions, was eager to travel to visit the beautiful gardens. She had to see now what she could accomplish alone.

The colours were there immediately without any effort and as if awaiting her closed eyes. The noise blotted out any other sound, even the screech owl in a nearby tree. She began to float but soon became upright. Then she was turned face down but not by her own doing. This made her want to experiment and she willingly turned herself upright and slowed her pace until she felt in total command. The colours were changing and pulsating to the sounds which seemed to be part of her. As she looked down through the colours something shocked her which caused her to tumble aimlessly for a moment. She was naked. At first she panicked but slowly Matthew's words echoed around her. "You form your own impression."

Jenny slowly imagined a long flowing Grecian style garment in white with gold edging. When she looked again, her heart jumped to see the brilliant white folds trailing from her. There was no feel to the material, just a satisfaction in her newly found capabilities.

The colours and high pitched whistle started to fade, and in their place Jenny found herself in her beautiful garden but this time she was not flying, she was going at her own pace. Also she noticed other people taking little notice of her, just aimlessly floating about savouring the beauty around them. They were clad in various garbs and she felt quite elegant in her choice of raiment.

The question arose "If this is my imagination, why are other people here? I did not wish for company, although I don't mind them". She travelled on and came to a lake which was completely deserted. "Oh well" she thought, "that's another question for the archangel when I see him." She paused at the edge of the lake. This was a wonderful new experience, about being able to stop and start at will. A chill from the water blew across her spiritual body. At first she wished she had dressed herself in warmer clothing then realised she could do that right now. The next thought sent an even greater chill down her spine.

She remembered Mrs. Randle once telling her that there was no feeling of temperature in the spirit world and that if a chill was felt, it heralded the arrival of an evil presence. At the time Jenny had thought it of little consequence and dismissed the idea, but now, alone, she knew fear as she had never experienced.

Looking across the water she saw a figure on the opposite bank. "Where did that come from? It wasn't there before." She was stationary, hovering just above the ground thinking it better to leave this place, when she realised the figure was now at her side. The chill was wrapping its icy fingers all over her body.

Although the form did not speak, the thoughts were immediately planted in her mind. "You're new to this, aren't you?"

"Yes" the words did not come out.

"You need a guide my dear."

Jenny struggled to see the creature's face but it seemed a blur. "Who are you?" She thought the question and received a reply immediately.

"Someone to help you."

The lake had disappeared and was nothing more than an ugly bog. The grass which was once beneath her feet was now like sand, pulling, dragging her down. She felt the creature leering with content, and panic overwhelmed her. The sadistic cackling laughter seemed to echo through her brain. As she struggled to hold on to her strength of will, one name sprang to mind. "Matthew." Her whole being screamed his name. As she gradually lost all sense of her surroundings, she was vaguely aware of strong hands on her shoulders lifting, supporting until the chill had gone.

"Jenny! Jenny!" The voice was screaming almost hysterically.

"Matthew" Jenny felt the softness of her bed beneath her.

"No Jenny, it's me, Mother." Kate was in tears and frantically shaking the girl by the shoulders. "Wake up, oh please wake up. Look at me."

Jimmy appeared over her shoulder. "Gently Kate, she's back with us now." But his voice shook with emotion.

Kate sat on the bed and sobbed uncontrollably. "We thought you were dead." Jenny sat up slowly. "Oh Mum." she cuddled Kate as tears ran down her own face. "Why is it," the mother was still badly distraught and the words came out stilted. "what is causing these awful nightmares?"

"Nightmares? Oh, was I shouting again. Sorry Mum, and you Dad, I've woken you up again haven't I?"

Jimmy and Kate exchanged glances. "Look Jenny, why don't you try and go back to sleep and we'll talk about it in the morning." Jimmy slipped his arm round his wife as he spoke. She looked up at him, her face ashen. He gently led her back to their room but called to Jenny "Try not to have any more - um - bad dreams lass."

"OK. Dad, and sorry again."

Back in the comfort of their own bed, Kate snuggled close to Jimmy. "I hate to say it."

"Say what?" Jimmy kissed her tenderly.

"She didn't have these--"

"What, nightmares?" Jimmy thought he was finishing the sentence for her.

"Call it what you will. But she only had them after she met Matthew."

"Um." Jimmy was thoughtful. "You're right you know love. But she seems so happy with him. Perhaps it's just the excitement of it all."

"Not to produce THAT. You saw her face this time." Kate shuddered.

Jimmy thought for a moment. "It's a big upheaval in anyone's life, to meet someone, perhaps she's in love, and don't forget she's not had many friends. Perhaps she's sensitive. After all she's always kept to herself, we didn't know what was going on in that head of hers."

"And we don't now. "Kate had stopped crying. She turned her face up towards her husband. "Do you realise something?"

"What's that?"

"I've never heard you open up like that. Ever. Something's changing us and I don't like it." She was very uneasy. Jimmy stroked her hair and said "Shall we tell her, you know, everything?"

"Let's play it by ear, and see." Kate settled down, but one ear was cocked ready for the next horrendous unearthly scream.

"I've just got to find Matthew." Jenny wanted to know what had happened, and she wanted to know now. So many questions needed to be answered. Who was the fiend? Was it one of the entities she had been warned about? Did they come any worse? Could it have killed her? How could it? Her brain was racing. "Matthew will know."

She closed her eyes and willed him to be with her but her brain was tormented and the colours swirled like an agitated kaleidoscope. The noise reached a deafening high pitched shrill. Faces zoomed in as if to collide with her face, then they would sweep off in any direction. Not nice faces. If the entity had shown its face, she felt it would have looked like one of these, or all of them. The pinched pointed little masks with pinpointed eyes, the lips stretched back over yellow teeth in a gruesome grimace. "Open your eyes." the order was almost snapped at her. She could not see Matthew but felt the reminder must have come from him. So she did as she was bid and opened her eyes. "I suppose I'll have to wait until I see him in the flesh." Then the thought of him holding her to him took over her being, and she smiled to herself. "Well, maybe that's better after all."

She just dozed on and off until morning not feeling it was safe to wander again tonight.

Chapter 6

Jimmy had already left for work when Jenny came down the stairs the following morning.

"Morning Mum."

Kate poured a cup of tea and handed it to her daughter. "Your dad and I wanted to have a word with you, together, that is, we are a bit worried about you." Her voice trembled and her hand was shaking.

"I'm I alright Mum, don't worry about me."

"But we are worried, very worried. You're not going out tonight are you, only we could talk then, after dinner."

"I'm seeing Matthew. I think he really likes me Mum." Jenny was thinking of his kiss.

"That's just it dear, we, I mean I, - - well, I was wondering if you shouldn't see him so much, for a while anyway." Kate stirred her tea as if to keep a focal point.

Jenny was on the defensive. "I've only been out with him twice!"

"Been out." Kate echoed. "Been out, you only go for a walk every time."

Jenny didn't feel comfortable with this conversation so she gulped down her tea, grabbed her bag and said "I'll miss the bus, see you later." She planted a quick kiss on her mother's head and was gone.

Mrs. Randle may not have been the most accurate medium in the business but she dabbled a little and could have had deeper insight into the 'other world' as she called it if she had opened her mind, and not given such a high regard to the practical things in life. Much of what she churned out was what she had read and not from personal experience, although that's what she would have you believe.

Jenny wanted to hear more about the chill factor, and although she knew Matthew would give her a perfectly informative explanation, she didn't want to wait for it, and she felt there wouldn't be any harm in getting another angle. This was all so new and exciting, if not scary, but that would sort itself, that she didn't realise how she was rushing headlong into an unknown world. Matthew had warned her to pace herself, but it was so difficult. "So much to learn."

When lunch time came, she waited for Mrs. Randle to get settled, then calmly said "That thing you were saying the other day, about cold chills, there was a programme on the telly about it. "She had to lie a little to protect her own self.

"Really!" Mrs. Randle's eyes opened wide. "I'm sorry I missed that. What channel was it on?"

Jenny thought quickly. "I didn't notice, but it was saying all the things you did. You know, about when an evil presence is there- "

"The room goes cold." Mrs. Randle wanted to appear knowledgeable so she finished the sentence.

"Yes. All about that." Jenny waited expectantly.

"Did they cover cold spots?"

"Um - I don't think so. What cold spots?" Jenny was hedging.

"Oh, I'm surprised they didn't, perhaps it will be in another programme."

"Yes, could be. What are they exactly, these---"

"Cold spots? Well, in certain places, say in a room of a house, you can feel it."

Jenny looked as blank as she could. "Feel it?"

"Yes. The air is cold. Chill. Horrible. You can walk through it but if you stand still where it is, it's not a pleasant feeling."

"Is that the same as when a presence comes into the room?"

Mrs. Randle paused. She was being pressured and felt somehow this girl knew more than she was letting on. Perhaps she knew more than she did herself. She straightened in her chair. "Well sort of. You could say that that is a moving one and the cold spot is always in one place." Jenny had a strong feeling the woman was making it up as she went along and whether or not she was right didn't matter too much. It did make sense and she would find out from Matthew. She'd just have to be patient, after all she would see him this evening.

Kate had prepared the evening meal in good time, Jimmy was home and they all sat down to eat.

"What time is Matthew coming?" Kate made it sound as casual as possible but Jenny wasn't fooled.

"Same as usual I expect. About seven I should think." And she thought "After the third degree though."

When they had finished the delicious apple pie, Jenny got up saying, "I'll do the dishes Mum, before I get washed and changed."

Her mother's hand went up to halt her. "All in good time. I can do them. But first Jenny we do have to talk to you, I did say this morning. "

Knowing there was no escape, she reluctantly sat down again.

"Go on then. What's all the fuss about?"

"Jenny" her mother was astounded. "You see, that's not like you. You were never insolent before."

"Before? Before what?"

Kate looked to Jimmy for advice. He put his hand over hers and looked at his daughter.

"Jenny, I saw something last night, I don't know what it was, but I didn't like it. It frightened your mother and we never want to see it again."

Jenny looked from one to the other and gave a little laugh. "What ARE you two on about? I had a bad dream didn't I? What more is there to say?"

"You didn't look like you." Kate almost screamed the words out, and Jimmy stroked her hand for reassurance.

He reached out with his other hand to Jenny. "Your face."

"What about my face? Is somebody going to tell me?"

Kate said in a very controlled voice "It's not the first time. When we hear that awful noise, it's like---"she turned to Jimmy "how would you describe it Jim?"

"Like an animal almost, only it's not. It's a horrible howl mixed with a scream, it goes through you."

"And your face," Kate grimaced at the thought" is distorted, your lips are pulled back in a snarl, and your eyes seem very small. Your hair seems to stand on end."

Jenny's hands went up to her face. What she was hearing was not unlike the images she had seen after her terrifying experience in the quicksand. Horror spread across her paled skin. "I looked like that?"

"Yes, yes dear," Kate grabbed her hand pulling towards her. "Now do you see why we are worried?"

"Yes, yes I do." Jenny smiled faintly at them both. She couldn't confide in them to reassure them she had to get this under control and she was rather worried about the physical changes that were occurring.

"It's only happened recently." Kate was trying not to put Jenny's back up again by mentioning Matthew's name.

"I know what you are saying "Jenny thought she would make her point first."But believe me, Matthew is a good person. He has nothing to do with this."

She got up and went to change.

"Did I say he had?" Kate asked Jimmy.

"You didn't." replied Jim. "But in a way, she did didn't she?"

Much as Jenny would have liked to have helped her mother clear up, she felt under extreme pressure and couldn't get out of the house quick enough. "To the protective wings of my archangel Gabriel." She relaxed at the thought. "I wonder what he will do tonight, and will it be physical or spiritual? But according to him, what's the difference?" She felt a thrill at the prospect of his body being close to her own and longed for the intimacy she felt was just around to corner. She could contain herself in the house no longer, so as soon as she was ready she went downstairs and said to her parents "I'll wait for Matthew by the gate, don't worry, I'll be fine." And the door closed as the words died on Kate's lips "Don't go far, it looks like --- rain" she finished to herself.

Chapter 7

Matthew met Jenny with a brief smile which faded almost immediately. They walked briskly in silence until they once again reached the wall.

"You don't have to tell me" Matthew began "they're playing with you, trying to frighten you, but it's all to get at me."

"You look so angry tonight." His fierceness saddened her.

"I am, but not with you." He fell silent.

"Who was it?"

"Oh, just some of the pranksters I warned you about," he tried to make light of it but his voice revealed his inner feelings. He held her close. "The last thing I want is to put you in danger. You are very precious to me." She snuggled into his chest.

"Mum and Dad said I didn't look like me, when they woke me."

"They saw! We must try and not let that happen again."

She almost whispered, "How can we do that?"

"You will become more experienced, you are progressing at a terrific speed but this is something we expected?"

She looked into his face. "Can you explain the 'we'? Whose we? Your people?"

"All in good time. First let me show you what many are capable of." She was eager for him to explain anything, and knew he would feed her the knowledge as he thought fit. She nodded.

"Remember me telling you how some people can recall everything they have dreamt?"

"Oh yes" she agreed, "I remember."

"Well, some can actually travel around at will."

"Like I've been doing." Jenny thought she understood fully.

"No, not exactly, you started off in your imaginary surroundings, with things how you would like them to be, until the beings took over."

"I'm not quite with you."

He smiled now. "Some can travel to actual places on earth. It was suspected during the war, that these 'walkers' could learn enemy secrets and then when awake feed the information back to their own country's military."

"NO!"

"Do you see the difference?" He eyed her quizzically.

"Yes, but could I do that?"

"Why not, in time." He let the idea sink in then continued, "You asked me how I knew of such a small place as South Lawn." His head inclined in the direction of the hamlet. "Well, during the last war there was a well known figure, a dictator, who had, shall we call it an affiliation with a certain lady who lived over there."

"Really!" Jenny's eyes were wide open in wonder.

"Need I tell you more? We wanted to learn all we could, and so a couple of 'walkers' used to keep an eye on his movements here."

"Don't tell me, you were one of them. No wait a minute, you wouldn't have been born then, or was that in a previous life?"

"You're learning quickly. But don't forget life is continual. A previous bodily form is more precise."

"What was your name?" Jenny thought of the most detailed questions.

"Can I just say that I was a very well know general?"

Jenny laughed "Do I have a choice?"

"Not really. The name is unimportant, but yes, I was one of them."

"Did he know, this dictator?"

Now it was Matthew's turn to laugh. "I should hope not. It would have rather spoiled the operation don't you think?"

"I suppose so, but fancy such a thing," she was still in awe of this new information. Was there no end to it?

Kate could not settle to anything. Jimmy tried to calm her, but she kept looking out of the window willing Jenny to return. She really wished Matthew had never come into their lives and yet he seemed a good person.

"I know I keep saying the same thing, "she sat down opposite Jimmy, "but it always comes back to it. She didn't start these awful dreams until she met him."

"But Kate love, it could be just chance, he can't have anything to do with it."

"I know that really." Kate sighed and fiddled with a cotton hanging from her apron. "The silly thing is, Jenny's so happy, so different, and in such a short time too. I don't want her hurt."

"Nobody wants her hurt." Jimmy wanted to ease his wife's burden but didn't know what else he could do, apart from listen. Kate had a mother's instinct that something was amiss but confused with the girl's elated state. If only she could get to the bottom of it. She almost dreaded the nights after the last episode, but she had no idea what she was up against.

"Are you warm enough?" Matthew hugged Jenny to him, "We should have come up in the car tonight.

"I've never seen your car, you always come for me on foot."

"That's easy, I always park it at a friend's place. Your cottage is on rather a nasty bend, so it's safer. Anyway I like to pass the time of day with Graham."

"Matthew?"

"Um, what is it?"

Jenny wondered if her lecture was over for tonight. "Where you come from, your planet or whatever it is, what's it called, and where is it?"

"You mean my space area. What would you like to call it?"

"But hasn't it got a name already?" This wasn't the reaction Jenny expected.

"What is a name? It doesn't mean anything."

"Well of course it means something, we have names for everything."

"O.K. Let me make it as easy as I can." He thought for a moment.

"What do you call a little insect that lives in a hill?"

"You mean an ant?" Jenny was still at a loss.

"You call it an ant." Matthew paused. "Does the ant know it is an ant?"

"Well no, it probably has a different language, or mean of communication."

"Good. You are making this easy."

"I am?"

Matthew went on. "So it carries a big white thing about."

"An egg." Jenny jumped in. "Oh I know, I call it an egg but the ant doesn't." This was becoming quite comical.

"Right. And what would a French person call it? Un Oeuf. A Japanese, a Dutch, shall I go on?"

"Oh, so we all have different name for the same thing but we all know what we mean." This seemed quite simple after all.

"Right. But does the ant need a name for the egg? Does it need a name for itself? It has the instinct and understanding of what is expected without calling it anything. A bee collects nectar to make honey. It knows what to do. But it doesn't know the name honey."

"Have we veered a little from why your space area doesn't have a name?" Jenny thought she was being clever now.

"Not at all. We know where it is and what it is and we do not waste communication on trivia so why give it a name?"

"You haven't told me where it is."

Matthew thought for a moment. "Let's leave that for now, just think of somewhere out there not too far away. In fact much nearer than you think."

"Alright." Jenny would have to settle for that for now, but she knew in time all would be revealed.

"But to accommodate your mortal needs my little elfin, think of a name so that you can refer to it."

Jenny though for a moment and then brightened "You took me through that beautiful garden, so I shall call your home Eden."

"Sounds as good as anything." Matthew looked towards the sky. "Time to go, we don't want to get wet and the sky looks a bit dark." He helped his love to her feet, and as they walked back to the village he said "I will do all I can to keep the bad forces away from you and there are others who will help you."

"Who helped me last night?"

"Would a couple of my friends be explanation enough for now?"

"Yes" said Jenny "but try not be too far away."

They reached the cottage and Jenny asked Matthew to join her for a drink before leaving.

"I'll just say Good night to your parents, but then I must be off, oh and Jenny, I wouldn't travel too far tonight. Give me chance to put a bit of protection around. Trust me." He kissed her, lightly at first followed by the passion she had known the night before.

"I love you my little elfin."

"And I love you, my archangel Gabriel. I'll do as you say."

Chapter 8

Over the weeks that followed Matthew was a regular visitor to the cottage. His relationship with Jenny was developing into a deep and lasting affection and it was clear to all that they were very much a couple. Much to Kate's relief, the dreams seemed to have stopped. There had been a couple of little sessions, but nothing as frightening as the previous and both parents slipped into a safe feeling that things were, at last, going to be alright.

Matthew had been guiding Jenny on the astral plane until she had reached levels higher than most with her experience time. He rarely left her unattended and protected her with his growing love which formed a shield around her. His friend Graham was always at hand, and Jenny now realised why they were such friends on earth. They had been born as twins previously and maintained the bond.

By Christmas, six months had passed and Jenny realised just how much she had experienced since her birthday. She never questioned her destiny and never felt tempted to divulge any of her secrets to anyone other than those she travelled with. She still saw her colours and heard her white noise, but these were now part of her eternal existence.

They were decorating the Christmas tree together when Jenny asked Matthew if her white noise was the same as was referred to in space.

"With not actually hearing what you hear, it's difficult to say." He swung a silver bauble slowly so that the light reflected off its many facets.

"You see" he said "white noise has no preferred frequency, from anything. It has random variation and really is a mathematical concept."

"I shouldn't have asked?" Jenny grinned at him. "But I can't stop asking things, I can't soak up enough information, I want more."

"There's nothing wrong with that, but did I answer your initial question?"

"I think so." Jenny said.

"Well just to confuse you even more, there is also pink noise, but you don't hear so much about that."

"Well," Jenny put a star on the top of the tree, "one thing is for sure, my white noise is blue, the most vibrant heavenly blue." She draped some angel hair over his fair locks, "So explain that one."

"It's different, but then you are."

"You'll be telling me next I'm from your place, Eden."

He was silent, toying with a length of tinsel.

"Matthew. I'm not." Then a realisation hit her. "I can't be."

"Why?"

"Because you said your people had, now what were the exact words 'total recall of all lives' wasn't that it? And I can't remember any previous ones. So I can't be one of your lot." Self satisfied she sat back smiling.

"You make the mistake of thinking there are no more than us."

"Eh?"

"Time for another explanation." Matthew tossed the tinsel to her. "America."

She shrugged "What about it?"

"Who settled there a couple of hundred years ago?"

"Do you mean English people?"

"I do. And who settled in Canada?" He waited for her reply.

"The French mostly."

"Mexico?"

"The Spanish."

"Right. So on one continent you have several different nationalities. Nobody bothers that they have come from different places. It is the accepted thing. That is on one bit of earth. So think of the planet as a whole."

"You mean there are different races, or aliens rather, that have come here and settled, or just spending a few lives here. Is that what you are trying to tell me?"

"Why are you so surprised? You accept me, and you know I am not alone. In fact it would be harder to identify anyone who is a true earthling, if there are any now."

"But why do we look the same, well mostly?"

Matthew gave her the kind of look a teacher gives a pupil when he wants to say "You should know that."

Jenny eyed him equally, tormenting him with her silence until she was ready.

"Well, let me see now," she collapsed in a fit of relaxed laughter, "oh I can't tease you for long. The answer is of course that we merely inhabit these bodies. They are as they are now, regardless of their evolution," she drew breath, "how am I doing?"

"Fine. Finish it off."

"So, we only look like the vehicle we are driving at the time." She hurried the last words feeling very pleased with herself.

"Very good." He applauded. "Now come here and give me a down to earth kiss."

They embraced for what felt like an eternity, although it was over too soon as Matthew held Jenny at arm's length.

"Jenny, my little elfin" he began "I know you have much to learn, and we are able to share our time away from our mortal trappings, but there is something else I would love very much."

"What is it? Jenny asked in a whisper.

"I want to marry you."

Jenny should have been prepared for this but Matthew had timed it beautifully and caught her off guard.

Before she could reply Matthew continued "Do you think your parents would agree? They seem to like me."

Jenny looked directly at him. "I haven't given my answer." Then she threw herself into his arms saying "Yes, yes, oh yes please, of course they like you."

"When will they be back?" He was eager to get the seal of approval and announce to the world she was his.

"Not long now, they only went down to help trim the church."

"Good. But before they do, there is something I must ask of you. We need your help, in fact we are being called in from all over."

Jenny was serious when she saw the expression on his face.

"You're using the 'we ' again."

"Sorry. Jenny, have you ever heard of the 'helpers'?"

"No, I don't think so."

Matthew sighed deeply. "Some people, whether in earthly form, in spirit or elsewhere in the universe are known as 'helpers'."

"I take it they help people." Jenny wondered where this was leading.

"Well yes, but especially those who have just passed from one life to another. You see some don't take it very well and need comfort."

Jenny frowned. "You mean they don't just accept it?"

"Why should they? Some of them have thought only of a physical existence all the while they have lived it. So it comes as a bit of a shock."

"You said you needed my help. Am I a helper?"

"Not really. But if there is a major disaster on earth or any planet where there is life, the obvious thing is you get a deluge of passing overs. The 'helpers' sometimes call for assistance. I wouldn't ask you to go anywhere away from earth yet, but if you could come with me tonight, we are required."

"This is a new one." Jenny pondered to let it sink in. "Where exactly, and why don't we go now?"

"It's over in the east, and we will go in our earth dark time when we do not have to explain being asleep. Help is being called from each time zone, therefore it is continual."

"Have you done this much." Jenny accepted every fact without question. "Quite a bit, it depends on the need you see."

"I take it we will travel at will, and we will go together." Jenny couldn't think of any other way but felt the need to ask.

"We have no option. I could go quicker but that would leave you trailing, and you couldn't cope alone, not yet."

"Tell me how you travel quicker, is it just a matter of speed? Is this the light wave you mentioned?"

The sound of the door being opened halted the conversation. Kate and Jimmy hurried in, welcoming the warmth from the blazing fire. "Shouldn't be surprised to see a flake of snow." Jimmy rubbed his hands before the flames.

"Would you like a hot drink?" Jenny was already on her feet and making her way to the kitchen.

"Oh that would be lovely, thank you." Her mother beamed at her. The girl looked radiant tonight. "She's in love ". Kate smiled to herself and then to Matthew who had been studying her closely.

When Jenny came in with a tray laden with tea and biscuits, he took it from her, placed it on the table and slipped his arm around her. He faced the parents and without a moments hesitation said "Kate and Jimmy, it would be a great honour for me if you would consent to Jenny becoming my wife." Kate's hands covered her mouth and her eyes glistened. Then she opened her arms and embraced them both. Sobbing with emotion she said "Look after her Matthew, and may you both be very happy." She kissed Jenny many times and only let her go for Jimmy to take over, hug his daughter and shake hands with his future son in law.

"Tea doesn't seem quite the right thing now" Jimmy patted Matthew on the shoulder then put his arm around his wife.

"Tea will warm you both up." Jenny started to pour out. "You are happy for us aren't you?"

"Of course we are dear. Where will you live?" Kate was being practical.

Jenny laughed. "We haven't even discussed that Mum. Matthew only asked me just before you came home, but we will sort something."

"There are many plans to make," Matthew was relieved at the response and he wanted to make Jenny his own without delay.

Kate sat down and took the tea handed to her. "So you haven't named the day?"

"Not yet." Matthew answered first. "What do you think ladies?"

"How about Easter." Jenny felt this appropriate. Engaged at Christmas and married at Easter."

"How about tomorrow?" Matthew laughed. "Only joking" he assured Kate.

"I should think so, she's got to have a proper wedding and there is so much to arrange."

"Well, that'll keep you busy for a while." Jimmy smiled but secretly hoped it would clear Kate's head of the apprehensions which had been on the surface lately.

"I know. On your nineteenth birthday in June. June's a lovely month." Kate felt that would be adequate time for everything to be just right, and she felt an urge not to rush it.

The two newly engaged people looked at each other and nodded in agreement. "Sounds a very sensible idea, Mother." Matthew emphasised the last word. Kate pretended to be vexed but instead actually laughed and said "Enough of that. Kate it is and Kate it always will be to you."

Later as Jenny saw Matthew to the door, he whispered "See you soon, we've work to do, and I'm sorry but it may not be pleasant."

"As long as you are there, I will cope." She waved into the darkness as he disappeared from view.

Chapter 9

Graham was at Matthew's side when Jenny floated from her sleeping body. They greeted her, all quickly applied appropriate appearance and were away. Matthew had her firmly by one hand and Graham the other as they rushed at high speed towards their destination. "Seems funny travelling like this again" Graham's thought reached them both. Jenny directed her reply to him. "How do you normally go?" Matthew came between them mentally. "We haven't covered that yet. Please there is little time, we must prepare you."

Although no speech was used the conversation was just as vivid. "The people who are dying, leaving their bodies, will be distraught as this is a disaster." Matthew was as brief as possible. "When people have been ill and death is expected, they have already geared themselves to it."

"It is often a relief "Graham added.

Jenny nodded.

"These poor souls, which is what they are now, have had no adjustment time beforehand." Matthew continued. "They would have been going about their business and the disaster struck."

"What was it?" Jenny's question floated in the air.

"Sorry" Graham said, "a flood, those that lived have lost everything, the ones we will help will be just as distraught."

Matthew hurried the instructions. "They may not realise they have left their bodies. They will need comforting just as if they were still alive."

Graham added, "You will even see helpers giving them clothes and food, because that is what they think is needed."

"Not real ones though?" Jenny wanted to be sure.

"Of course not. We are only feeding their minds with what will comfort them." Matthew hastened to add. "Don't forget Jenny, we can only help those in transition, don't try to go to those not yet passing."

Graham directed to a point almost beneath them. "Here we are." and all three descended to the chaos below. Matthew held up a hand.

"Word of warning. Beware the evil ones. They revel in this sort of thing. They will be here."

Nothing could not have prepared Jenny for the sight that lay before her. The painful sorrowing of the tormented dead filled the atmosphere around them. Souls floated aimlessly, subconsciously looking for relatives. One clung to Graham immediately. The look of utter horror on its face sent a shudder through Jenny, but she was pulled away by a helper to a baby. The lifeless body was submerged in the water, trapped. As she watched, the little spirit form rose crying frantically. Instinctively she wrapped her arms around it and held it close to her. The vulnerable little trace of existence had no sooner found a new life, than it had been snatched away. A hand rested upon her shoulder. "I'll take it now, it is from our family." The elder had obviously been sent to take over one of its offspring. Just as Jenny was about to hand it over, Matthew appeared at her side. "Don't." There was no doubt as to the order. Other helpers gathered and drove the elder away. It changed form into the familiar pinched face with lips stretched over its yellow teeth. With a sickening laugh it sped away.

Jenny clutched the child to her. "I'm so sorry." She was angry at herself for being so naive. "I was warned" she tried to explain to the helper nearest to her who assured her, "Don't worry, it happens to all of us at first. We have to be as clever as they."

Graham was trying to comfort a man who would not accept his passing. He was determined to get back to his family. He seemed happier when he met up with his wife and son, but Graham had the job of convincing him they had all perished together.

A female helper, Marie, stayed with Jenny as they gathered as many children as possible together. "There will be protectors arriving shortly to take them on. They will be safe with them."

"It's a good job you know who they are." Jenny looked around her. "When I think of how I nearly ---" "Don't think." Marie assured her. "We are used to it, we are on guard all the time."

"Do you always do this? I mean, you couldn't just be doing this sort of thing, and nothing else." Jenny shuddered.

Marie smiled. "Helpers do all sorts, people are in transition all the time, not only on your earth. We can be called anywhere."

"But isn't it depressing?"

"Don't think of it as dying. These will all be back on their own space areas soon. All waiting for a repositioning, or birth as you call it."

Jenny was instinctively rocking the baby in her arms and she realised it had stopped crying. Marie peeped at its tiny face, then turned to her.

"You see, you are a natural, she feels safe with you."

"Oh, I hadn't even given a thought to what sex it was. A little girl. I wonder what her name was." Then remembering a previous lesson she added "Oh you don't bother with names do you?"

Marie smiled "That's only in our space area. Give her a name of your own if you like."

"Can I?"

Marie moved away to another helper but said "Why not?"

Jenny looked at the children gathered at her feet. "Right" she mustered them, "we are going to play a little game while we wait."

They clamboured to her still needing comfort and motherly love. "Does anyone know this little baby's name?" They all shook their heads.

"Right, shall we give her one?" They all nodded, brightening a little. Jenny caught sight of Marie returning with protectors of the eastern races so she hurried. "How about giving her my name. Would that be nice?" The all nodded again.

It never occurred to Jenny that their language was different and that they wouldn't understand. It was some time later when she reflected on the events, that the truth dawned. They had all been communicating by thought alone and Matthew's remarks that words were unnecessary held meaning.

The helpers watched the departure of the children but it was seeing little baby Jenny taken that upset the older Jenny the most.

"How's she doing Marie?" Graham's thought almost made them jump.

"Excellent. You can bring her any time Graham."

Matthew appeared. "Thanks for taking her under your wing, not easy the first time is it?"

"I have to go, I'm needed." Marie brushed Jenny's arm. "I've enjoyed meeting you, I will see you soon." and she was with another group immediately.

Matthew moved closed to Jenny. "I can't go yet, but this was enough for you for one session."

Jenny showed her disappointment. "I am to go back?"

Graham will take you part of the way. Then follow the thin line of light which leads you back to your bodily form."

Jenny would much rather have stayed with her beloved, but knew better than to argue.

Matthew turned to Graham. "Half way should be enough. Do me a favour though."

"Of course, what is it?"

"This disaster has rather rushed things, although it's given Jenny a leap forward, but I haven't covered the connecting light yet. Could you explain on the way back?"

"Consider it done." He moved away for the two to say farewell.

Jenny's last view of her future earth husband, was watching him comfort an old man who thought he was still alive.

Kate peeped in to Jenny's room out of curiosity. She had been woken by the sound of a baby crying and had to find out what it was. The door creaked slightly as she moved up to the bed. Before her lay her daughter in a deep sleep. Her arm was outside the covers in a crooked position and she was rocking it gently and cooing. "She must be dreaming, probably made the noise without knowing" she thought. Not wanting to spoil this peaceful scene, she crept silently back to her room.

"Was she alright?" Jimmy wanted to know.

"Seems fine. Never seen her look so calm."

"Did she cry out?" he whispered.

"Must have done. Anyway, everything's alright. Go to sleep."

If Kate had known what was in store for Jenny, she would not have rested so easily.

Jenny started the communication. "I always thought the thing that tied your spirit to your body was a silver chord. That's what I've always read."

Graham was travelling very close as if to protect her.

"No, it's the light line. That is what the evil entities try to break so that you cannot return."

"But surely, it could be interrupted? What if something got in the way?" Jenny was always ready with a question.

Graham paused. "It's not light as you know it, not quite. Let's say you shone a torch. It would send out a beam of light, imagine a narrow beam for now."

"OK."

"Now, if you held a piece of card in front of the torch, the light would not go through it, would it?" Graham waited.

"No. It would stop. Is that what you mean?"

"Yes. But our light lines aren't quite the same. If something tried to get between you and your body, the light would bend around it."

Jenny was amazed. "So it wouldn't be cut, or stopped?"

Graham realised what Matthew had told him, about this girl being a quick learner. She certainly was an easy pupil. He went on "You can have many bends during one travel. As the light goes round the obstacles, it snakes but is still connected."

Jenny was one step ahead, again. "So, how can the bad things cut it?"

"Ah," Graham didn't want to go too deeply, better leave that for Matthew "There are many devious ways."

"Tell me."

"You know enough for now, Matthew will take over where I left off." Jenny knew, yet again that there was no point in pursuing the fact.

"We're almost where I leave you. Will you be alright on your own?" Graham wasn't too happy at the prospect. There were many forces active and he felt she was still very vulnerable, and he felt responsible to his friend. "I'll be fine," she reassured him. "Are you going back to the disaster?"

"Yes but not by this means."

"This is something else I will have explained isn't it?"

"It is. Travel safe." and his being was no more.

Jenny followed her light line at speed. She had not wanted to leave the disaster scene, but now she felt an urge to return to the safety of her earth home. Many questions still were uppermost in her mind. She was determined to make her new fiancé explain how he and others travelled. Also she had a burning desire to know where she had come from. What part of space and why he had been delegated to guide her if she was not from Eden.

"I thought you would have been back by now." The thought in her mind made her jump. She realised Graham was again at her side travelling at her speed.

"Oh, you startled me." She had been lost in her own thoughts and wondered how long he had been in her presence. "Why did you come back?"

"I wasn't needed any more. But just as well I came, you were well off your guard then weren't you my pretty one?" It occurred to Jenny that Graham had never been this familiar. Friendly yes, but she was Matthew's and Graham held his previous twin in high esteem. A warning shot through her mind although she tried not to make it obvious.

"So are you taking me home?"

"We may as well travel together. I can protect you."

Then Jenny noticed something very important. He had no light line. She tried to clear her mind of all thoughts in case this being could tune in, for she didn't want it to suspect she had fathomed it. She was learning fast. This night had propelled her experience at such a force, she was able to deduce much without guidance.

"I may not go yet." She veered away slightly but it followed. "There are friends I have to visit on the way." He stayed closely at her side so she tried an experiment. She mentally thought of her colours and the high pitched whistle and directed them at him. Facing him she summoned all her love for Matthew and forced it at Graham's likeness. Instinctively she knew this was forming a protective shield around her, repelling the thing, and she rejoiced inwardly as she saw it retracting. Keeping up the force field she outstretched her hand and pointed straight between its eyes. "Get away from me. Do you think me that naive? Go back from whence you came and trouble me no more." She couldn't explain why she used such terminology, it just flowed out naturally. Did it matter? It worked. But she was not prepared for what now appeared before her and it took all her self control not to flinch before the sight. Graham's form was just over six feet tall, but gradually it grew until it towered over her, its grotesque head topping an animal's body. The yellow eyes bored into her as it exposed its fangs dripping saliva. The fur was matted and bare in places. Summoning all the power she could, the colours wrapped around her and concentrated into a point directed at the fiend. It let out a blood curdling howl, shrank to the size of a small dog, then was gone.

Jenny was trembling but proud she had not visibly flinched before the hideous thing. Fortunately Matthew's words had been foremost in her mind.

"You form your own impression, or the impression you are given. There are entities which can create an image and make you see what they want you to see." That, she was sure, is what had seen her through this visitation. What the thing actually looked like was of no consequence, and it had taught her to always be on her guard and not take anything for what it first appeared. Wasn't that one of her first warnings?

In a very short space of time, she was safely in her body, stirring in the comfort of her warm bed. Relief swept over her as she realised she was alone, and her parents were not at her bedside. "They couldn't have heard anything tonight," she mistakenly thought as she dozed lightly as the dawn appeared. Her thoughts turned to the poor victims of the flood as she realised she had total recall of the nights events.

Chapter 10

The Christmas season passed quietly with Matthew spending much of the time at the cottage. He had bought Jenny an engagement ring and everyone in the village congratulated the couple whenever they met.

"We ought to meet your parents." Kate ventured, "have they met Jenny yet?"

A fleeting glance was exchanged between the young couple.

"They are often away," Jenny said, but looking to Matthew for reassurance "aren't they?"

"Very true. I live with them, although they go abroad a lot and I think they like to feel someone is looking after their house, so it is a satisfactory arrangement."

Kate was in one of her 'finding out' moods. "I think Jenny said you lived over Charlbury way, isn't that right dear?"

Matthew didn't give time for a reply but said. "It's nearer to Woodstock actually, near Blenheim."

"Oh lovely, isn't that lovely Jimmy?" Kate tried to include her husband but he felt happier engrossed in his paper.

The wedding had been arranged for the Saturday nearest to Jenny's nineteenth birthday, which fell on a Monday. Kate tried to push it until the following week so that her daughter was actually nineteen, but succumbed under pressure. The Mr.and Mrs. Gavrielle to be, sensed the delay tactics but both decided they wanted the marriage to be as near to their first date as possible. So the date was fixed.

"So much to arrange" Kate would fuss and she would have been rather disappointed had she known that the pair would happily have married immediately without any of the trappings expected.

Although Matthew was elated at the thought of knowing Jenny would belong to him in the earthly form, he knew her progress was escalating at a speed where he would no longer be required. He hoped they could travel the galaxies together, and that she would still want him as much, when she learned the full truth about herself.

After the disaster, Jenny had demanded to know about the faster form of travel. She was standing by the low wall with Matthew both well wrapped up against the winter cold. The village looked like an oasis in the bleak landscape around them, very different to the summer when they first stood in the same spot.

"I think I have done remarkably well, especially on my own." Jenny's tone signalled 'no messing'.

"You have my little elfin," Matthew paused to kiss her. "But you haven't been tested to the full yet."

"Tested? What is this? An assault course?" She was far from amused.

"A very good name for it. You have fought off the minor entities because at your level that is all you will attract. The higher, more powerful ones would not consider you worth bothering with. They go for those of us who travel higher fields." He paused, knowing she would feel offended.

"Thank you."

"Don't take it to heart, think it through, it will make sense."

She looked at him unsmiling. "There are worse things? I've seen some pretty horrible ones you know, and beaten them, by will power alone."

"He held her hand tightly."Yes I know, but this is only the beginning."

She brightened a little. "Well, how about my next lesson, teacher?"

"A good idea" he said, a little relieved.

"Up to now," he began "you have travelled the colour and sound fields, you have travelled at speed, returning on your light line, but you have not yet travelled in instant thought."

"That's what you and Graham do?"

"And many others. It does depend a little on your space area base, but the concept is much the same."

"And the burning question. When do I get to do it? Will you teach me? Does it come naturally?"

"Wow." he laughed loudly, "You still ask many things at once."

The look of the young innocent girl returned. "I'm sorry." And she snuggled against him. He couldn't help thinking with some regret that she would not always be like this, but he knew events had to run their course.

"O.K. It works something like this. I am here but I want to get - over there." He pointed to a signpost at the road junction. So, in my bodily form I have to pick up this living tissue and physically take it over there. You don't want me to do it?"

"I think I can follow without the demonstration." Jenny was curt again.

"Hm. Well, remember I told you we exist without a bodily form, when we inhabit our space area?" He waited.

"Yes, I remember." her tone was softer now. She felt she had put in her place by his manner.

"We have no vehicle to transport, only our minds."

"You think it!" Realisation rushed into her brain. "Why didn't I work that out for myself?"

"Why should you? I have been purposely feeding you knowledge in small amounts. Don't feel disappointed that I had to lead you to the facts."

"I'm right then, aren't I?"

"Just about. You see, if I was moving in thought travel, I would think that position and be there in an instant." Matthew smiled. As usual she was making these explanations so easy for him to give. Too easy.

"And that is why you seem to disappear." It all seemed so clear, so logical prompting the next question.

"So, when can I do it, or is it only you people from Eden, just a minute, does it make a difference where I came from?"

"Oh no," Matthew said aloud. "I didn't want to touch on that yet." But continued "Yes it does make a difference, like I said, it depends on your space area."

"So," she emphasised." Can I or can't I?"

Very quietly he said, "Yes you can do it." knowing this was almost the final stage in the training. After this they would be almost equal, until she learned the truth and with that knowledge, left him far behind.

She couldn't wait to go to sleep that night. The urge to test this new step took over her whole being. It was as if something was driving her to reach a goal and nothing would stop her until it was achieved.

Both parents were aware of a change in her. No longer did they see the quiet little thing that didn't have friends, that scurried about like a mouse in its hunt for food. Before them blossomed a self assured young woman who knew her own mind and seemed to have a purpose of which they were not part. She was satisfied with Matthew's company to the exclusion of all others, including themselves almost.

"Just as well they're getting married," Kate thought whilst sewing the wedding dress, "she only seems happy when she is with him." She eyed the single bridesmaids dress. "There ought to have been at least four." It had been a problem getting Jenny to accept having one, and then reluctantly she agreed to her cousin Anne. "But after all," Kate stitched lace around the yoke, "who else could she have had? She hasn't any friends."

Jenny was determined it would work first time. Inexperience still prevailed, but this female was one who would only learn the hard way. She had learned to build up her protective shields and her thought power had increased so dramatically, it even frightened her a little.

Drifting into sleep she travelled up, pausing to take a peek into her parents' room. They were asleep.

"I wonder where they go "she thought, but was consoled by the fact that they would have little or no recollection of their journeys. They would awaken thinking they had dreamt, if they thought at all.

She rarely wandered aimlessly now, she had progressed at such a rate that she either visited people or places or would be called in as a 'helper'.

"Where shall I go?" she wondered "better not be too adventurous the first time."

She floated back to her own room. "I know. Our place." She concentrated hard on the low wall and imagined herself sitting on it. Nothing. She tried again. Still nothing. She became irate and although she repeated the experiment several times, she remained in her bedroom. In frustration she travelled at speed to the wall. Perhaps it would be easier to return, this being the first time. With every ounce of concentration she tried to imagine her room but she remained exactly where she was. The winter chill engulfed her, but she was experienced enough to know this was no weather condition. She looked around, searching the night for some indication of what was approaching. There it was. Standing by her wall. She tried the thought travel again in a vain attempt to frighten the being.

"Is this what you are trying to do, without much success?" The thought entered her brain as the form appeared on the opposite side of the road. It looked like a little old man, back bent, but with a leering look that went through her. She did not answer but stared at him unflinching. He reappeared on the wall, his cackling laughter echoing through the night.

"You don't recognise me in this form?" His question was more of a statement.

"Should I?"

"You wanted to know what I looked like." He appeared to be growing in stature before her. The back was straightening now, the hair becoming blond, the eyes taking on a deep blue hue she had only seen once before.

"Well," it asked, "which will you prefer on your wedding night. The choice is yours." If Jenny had been in her earthly form she would have been sick.

She was about to say his name, when caution took over. Which was the true image? If either. Searching for his light line, she felt relief as she saw it snaking out beyond him. Caution shouted again. This being could also have earthly form, but it didn't have to be Matthew. The tell tale chill was still there, so that settled it.

"You enjoy your little games don't you?" She projected the thought at the image in front of her.

"I'm sorry Jenny, it's part of the training. I can't stress how important it is never to drop your guard. But full marks, you were still wary."

"Do NOT be clever with me." She was still angry at the prospect of having been 'played with', especially by such an evil force.

"Jenny, I didn't want to do this. I have been putting it off."

"They why do it now? Or are you following instructions." She flounced away from him, a strong urge willing her from his presence as though switching off an electrical appliance. In an instant she was in her bed.

"Yes." The anger had gone. Now she was jubilant. "I've done it."

She lay comfortably computing everything in her mind. The answers were there, but always just out of reach. Why couldn't she thought travel at the first attempts? Lack of knowledge or experience seemed the obvious answer but it was only when she felt strong emotion, anger in this case that it happened. But the anger had not really been the trigger. It was the mental switching, the electrical power activating at the precise moment that had transported her in the blink of an eye. Strangely enough, there was something very familiar about it, as though this was not an initial training, but a short refresher course, which was why she was progressing so rapidly.

Matthew had explained how it took many lives to achieve self perfection. The general earthly belief focused on seven lives, but in fact that depended upon the source of an individual's space area. Some would take more, some less, plus the factor of which planet in which solar system was currently being visited.

Jenny mused upon these thoughts for a while but was aggravated by the missing links. Above all, she felt as though she had long term amnesia, that there was much others knew about her that had happened previously, about which she was still unaware.

"There is one way to remedy that" she felt quite belligerent "and I intend to do it without further delay, whether THEY like it not." She rolled over and drifted into a peaceful uneventful sleep.

Chapter 11

Everyone at Jenny's place of work was delighted at the news of her engagement. They knew Matthew well through his business connections with the firm, and the general feeling was these two they made the perfect couple.

Mrs. Randle was the first to give her junior worker a hug and wish her well.

"Of course, I knew." She almost preened as she eyed the ring. "The minute you two met, well, you could positively see the vibes. But them who am I telling? I know you will make each other happy, you were made for one another."

Jenny was rather relieved when George, her boss came to her rescue.

"OK, let's not embarrass the lass." He handed Jenny some contracts with a little wink. "Any chance of them today?"

"Of course, no problem" and she settled back at her desk to concentrate on her work.

Mrs. R. was not one to be put off so easily.

"Will you carry on working, for a while at least?"

Jenny looked up in surprise. "I should imagine so, why do you ask?" She wasn't short with the woman but felt this was out of the bounds of having anything to do with her.

"Well," Mrs. Randle gave a knowing shrug, "you never know, do you?"

"Don't I?" Jenny was now quite an expert in evasion.

The self professed medium didn't like brick walls. And this girl was solid. A good job her 'subjects' didn't close there minds like this or she would be out of business.

"For goodness sake." She took a deep breath

"Babies." There. She had been forced to say it and the words had no sooner left her mouth, than she wished she could have retracted them. Jenny put down her pen and stared at her.

"Mrs. Randle. I am not even married yet, but I'm sure things will happen in their proper time. However, if you have a vision you think is important, I'm sure you will waste no time in sharing it with me, and anyone else that happens to be interested."

The medium sat open mouthed for several moments, and only came back to her senses with the ringing of the telephone. When she had finished answering the call, she stared at the girl who was now deep in her work. Could this be the same mousy little thing she had nurtured for two and a half years? That one would never have dared speak like that. It occurred to her that maybe this was just growing up, or the self confidence of being a wife soon. But no, there was more to it than that.

"Poor Mrs. Randle." Jenny grinned inwardly," with her lack of talent, she'll never fathom it out."

A big event was on the horizon. Jenny was well accomplished in thought travel and had transported with Matthew and Graham to many earth locations. But now it was time for visits further afield.

"There's no good attempting too far a distance too soon." Matthew and Graham were in the latter's study, deciding on the first trip. Graham knew his friend was being practical, but also using delaying tactics.

"You can't put it off for ever. It's inevitable, and not fair to her."

"For God's sake man, my work will soon be finished, and then what? I'll be recalled. I'm marrying her in June. How can I let her know I will be snatched back?" Matthew was near to tears.

"There's a lot to do yet." Graham tried to console him.

"I know. But as soon as she gets up there, Eden she calls it, she'll soak it up like a sponge. The knowledge will be absorbed faster than I can feed it."

Graham poured him a drink. "You are terrified you won't be here long enough to marry her, aren't you?"

Matthew nodded his thanks and sipped his whisky. "The speed, I mean, it's only been about seven months."

"What did you expect?" Graham sat back and waited for Matthew to continue but in vain. So he decided to voice the other man's feelings for him.

"Jupiter, Mercury and Neptune were prominent, all sevens, it had to figure somewhere. She couldn't have taken seven years."

This prompted a response. "I know, I know." Then after a pause, "Do you know, I envy these earthlings, the ones who don't know destiny, or what is around the corner. At least they aren't tormented about it the same."

"You shouldn't have fallen in love whilst in earthly form."

"It's alright for you. They gave you Thomas, you couldn't fall for him. And I won't make a sick joke about that."

Graham pulled himself up in his chair. "Thanks for nothing. Never been that way inclined old chap, in any life."

They both mused for a moment then Graham asked "When is it, tonight?"

"Yes. I had better get going."

"She doesn't know?"

Matthew looked a little sheepish. "Yes, actually, she's been pestering me, so she knows where, and when."

"Good luck then. I'd join you, but three's a ---well, travel safe." The friends bid each other 'Good night' and each went about their individual tasks.

Jenny was beside herself with excitement. This would be the opening of a portal to explain the many unanswered questions racing through her head. She just knew it. Her parents were not surprised at her retiring early, she did every night, so to them, this was nothing unusual.

Hovering just above the house, she eagerly awaited Matthew's arrival. Within seconds he was there. He came very close to her and explained how they would travel away from the earth. This required a much greater 'switch' to escape the gravity.

"How far is it?" Jenny wanted all the details.

"Not far beyond the moon. You would never see it from earth as it is always hidden, travelling at the same speed, so the moon blocks it."

"So tell me, when the astronauts landed on the moon, one of them stayed in the capsule and went round it, didn't he." Jenny wanted to know why nothing had been mentioned of this planet she called Eden, they must have seen it.

"I won't be clever and say they were so busy looking at the far side of the moon, not to notice. The truth is, as you will see, the universe is filled with all sizes of rock, ours would be quite insignificant. And it isn't a planet."

Jenny didn't quite understand this yet but was so eager to see Eden she put it to the back of her mind for now.

Matthew made sure she was ready and together they switched. In a flash they were in her beautiful garden.

"This is it?" She looked around in wonderment. "But I've been here before."

"No. Not here."

"But it's the same. Oh wait a minute, you created the image before."

"And?" Matthew waited.

"You created it in a likeness of this?" Jenny hoped she was right, but a little doubt surfaced.

"Jenny, this is only as we want it to be. The area is barren. We exist here in mind, we do not need material things. You create you own surroundings for your own peace of mind. We are only in thought pattern but do not make the mistake of thinking this is not as real as tangible things."

This was not quite as Jenny imagined, and it was all a bit too much to absorb.

"It will all fall into place." Matthew assured her. "Do you feel up to meeting one of our mentors?"

"Oh yes please, how do we do that?"

Jenny felt herself being pulled forward. The garden image faded and she was facing a light so bright that soaked the surrounding space with a warm feeling of peace.

"My child." The soft gentle tone rang through her being. "You are progressing well, but be patient and you will learn much." She felt a caress across the top of her head almost like a blessing and her whole self glowed with a feeling of inner calm.

As the light faded, Matthew was again at her side. "Enough for the first visit I think." He was happier now, in the realisation that her training would take longer than he envisaged. This new mode had slowed her and he would be needed until her realisation was complete.

She nodded silently, overawed with the presence she had been privileged to encounter.

"We will travel to just beyond moon in thought, then revert to speed, for a while, I have something to show you." Matthew drew her to him. "Ready."

Again she acknowledged in silence.

"Did you hear anything?" Kate nudged Jimmy. He was snoring loudly and it would have been unlikely he would have heard anything.

"Um." he grunted as she woke him.

"Jimmy, it's too quiet."

"How can it be too quiet? Go back to sleep."

Kate pointed her small torch toward the clock. "Half past three. I'll just go and check, see if she's alright."

"Course she's alright. Stop fretting."

Kate was already putting her slippers on as she spoke, "I'd feel better."

Jimmy grunted again and tried to settle down, but inwardly wanted the reassurance his wife would surely bring. The mother crept into the little room and peeped at the sleeping form. At first she felt relieved at the silence, but then she realised it was too silent. There was no breathing sound. Concerned she crept closer to the bed until her face was almost on the pillow. The room felt completely empty, no presence, no warmth, just a void. Gently she laid a hand on Jenny's forehead and as she did so, the light from the landing flooded in behind her. Kate felt the warmth from the body flood up her arm.

"She's alright you see." Jimmy peeped over Kate's shoulder, then returned to his bed.

As she turned and buried her face in her own pillow, Kate wished she knew what was happening. But who could she ask?

Chapter 12

If Jenny thought she was knowledgeable, her journey back to her earthly form made her realise she knew very little. Although Matthew had touched upon life from other planets and galaxies, he had not gone into detail regarding their means of transporting.

"You understand how our kind have no use for words, names of people or places". Matthew had halted them near the moon.

"Yes I could sense it more than anything, when I was on Eden." Jenny was still in awe of this feeling.

"Well, not every life form is like that. Some communicate, not by thought, but sound. Only it isn't quite like your word system." He was a little relieved at her confusion. "Why I'm telling you this, is because we need to refer to certain space areas. I can think a certain location, but as you have never been you wouldn't be able to lock on to the image."

"I see why your lot are so advanced. Are you one of the highest in intelligence?" Jenny was still trying to sort her mind into order.

"Pretty well, as far as we know, of course. But let us get on. I won't confuse you with too many different kinds at once, but for the reason of what you are going to see I have to explain the creatures from Schyn which is just inside this solar system."

Jenny tried to take it all in without speaking until Matthew had finished.

"Right. On earth you have electricity running through your body. It works on impulses from the brain but cannot cause you to light up. It isn't that sort, although there is a theory that it actually lights up part of the brain. However, Schyn is a very highly charged electrical place, and the inhabitants are not only adapted to live there, they harness the electricity, turn it into light and travel in light spheres or on light panels."

Jenny cast a look at Matthew which said "Are you kidding?"

He smiled and continued. "You will see shortly. Let us travel in speed mode." They left the moon and headed towards the dark side of the earth. Suddenly, they saw a streak of light race across the heavens.

"That's the first." Matthew was not surprised. "When they are re-positioning any of their kind on earth, they bring them down this way. They take them back like it too."

"Would we call them shooting stars? If we could see them from earth." Jenny was looking round for more.

"The ones that are far enough from earth you might. But the ones that come near enough to drop or pick up, that's when you get a run of UFO sightings."

"Of course" Jenny was beginning to understand, strange as it was.

Matthew pointed to another streak and said "The papers will be full of it tomorrow."

"Was that a sphere or a panel?" Jenny said.

"Too far away to tell. We expected an influx about now because the sun is in an active phase. They pick up the electrical charges from the prominences, which is why they time the visits very carefully."

"Do they go to one particular place, or just anywhere on earth?" Jenny was looking for the next one.

"Anywhere. But you will be able to spot them now."

"Why, have they got antenna?" Jenny was enjoying this.

Matthew was glad to see her so happy. "No, not exactly."

"I knew I shouldn't have asked that. Go on."

"There's a group of them, over there look, "Matthew indicated then said "What do you know about lightning?"

Jenny paused. "It's electrifying." She was still enthralled by what she was experiencing.

"When lightning comes down, it looks for streamers going up."

Jenny stared at him. "From people, from the ones from Schyn. Is that what you are trying to say?"

"The streamers go up from trees, high buildings, and the Schynings. That's how they re-charge. The transporters always try to place them in a high risk area so it is on tap."

"I've seen lightning, fork lightning coming down, but I've never seen streamers going up I must admit." Jenny was a little uncertain but had to believe what Matthew was explaining.

"I'll show you when we get nearer to the earth." Several light panels silently zoomed past.

"It explains one thing." Jenny mused.

"Oh good. What would that be?"

"The UFO sightings." Jenny gave a little nod.

"Go on."

"Well, all the reports say that the lights can hover, then take off at great speed but don't make a noise."

"That's right. And now you know just how they do it."

"How do they drop and pick up?" The more Jenny was seeing and learning, the more she wanted to know.

"The spheres often make indentations. They can be blamed for the odd crop circle, although not all. But mostly this is where your stone circles come in."

"Like Stonehenge?" Jenny asked.

"A long time ago, a round panel came down there and was spotted by the locals." Matthew was still looking around for more activity. "Obviously, this was way before the space age, even before aircraft in the most primitive form. The locals thought it was one of the gods visiting. The Schynings took advantage of this and helped to erect the circle which is exactly the size of the light panel. It also explains the exact positioning of the stones in relation to the constellations. These travellers would come and go at will, stirring up beliefs in witchcraft and the like and revelling in the lack of knowledge which was protecting the truth. But, the earth in that place still holds the electrical energy left from these landings."

"Were all stone circles put up in the same way?" Jenny wanted all the answers before they reached earth which she noticed was not far off.

"No. The ones near us, The Rollright Stones were erected by man."

"How do you know?"

"On one visit, the landing was witnessed by a farmer who rushed to tell the nearby inhabitants. Some thought he was mad, some thought he had had a drop too much to drink. But a local coven of witches believed something strange had happened and erected the stones to what they thought would have been a correct position for a landing, the king stone is where they reckoned someone special was put down."

"We are slowing down." Jenny didn't want this journey to end.

"You wanted to see a streamer." Matthew pointed to a storm below them. A finger of fork lightning shot down to earth.

"I didn't see one."

"You won't at that speed." Matthew gently swirled her around until everything below them slowed until it was barely moving. As the next fork descended, they watched as a several streamers rose from a farmhouse, a telegraph pole and nearby trees. Their fingers reached up like pupils in class saying "Me miss." The down fork selected one of the upstretched tentacles and connected. Matthew swung them back to normal speed.

"How did you do that?"

He ignored the question and said "Did you like it?"

"It was wonderful. Oh look, the light panels, over there."

Matthew gave them a mere glance and said "As a finale, you may as well see the northern lights The sun's activity is playing havoc with the earth's magnetic fields right now, but the lights are worth a look, and you won't see them from down there."

Jenny gasped as she drank in the swirling hues illuminating all around her.

"They are almost as good as my colours." She marvelled at such natural beauty. "Don't you miss things like this on Eden?"

Matthew laughed. "Why should I? I can see these."

Back in her bed, Jenny tried to recapture every single experience of the night. And what a night. She was again overcome by the strange feeling that although she had been shown things beyond her wildest imagination, she had experienced it all before, and Matthew knew it.

Chapter 13

The wedding was fast approaching. Kate, being allowed more or less a free hand, took full advantage of overseeing every single arrangement. Jenny would have taken a more active part, had she not been engrossed in her 'out of body' activities. Her mother was not leaving any stone unturned in her preparation of her daughter's big day. Mrs. Samson in the village was making the cake, and Janet Cox, one of Jenny's old classmates, was going to do the flowers. Just having started her own business, she welcomed the trade, and, according to all accounts had a natural flair for it. Kate had finished Anne's dress and hoped desperately it would fit. Jenny's would only have the final touches just before the day "In case of any ins and outs" as Kate put it.

She had also made her own outfit, a dress and full length coat to match in a vibrant blue. She didn't really know why she had settled on that material, it was very bright, but Jenny had insisted on it.

"It will suit you Mother" she had persuaded, "you will be stunning."

The wedding would take place at the local church, and the nearby Beaconsfield Hall had been hired for the reception, with a modest spread from a local caterers in Milton. The bride and groom had toyed with the idea of going to the Shaven Crown, a hotel in the centre of the village, but both Kate and Jimmy were from simple stock and this wasn't really their taste.

"I only hope it's posh enough for his people." Kate was wondering now if the right choice had been made. Jimmy was happy with the arrangements but didn't want Matthew's folks to look down on them.

Kate was peeling potatoes at the kitchen sink and Jimmy was at the door scraping mud off his boots.

"We've only met 'em once." he called out.

"Yes I know, but they don't seem short of a penny or too."

"Well, that's how we've planned it now, and anyway, there won't be that many of us." Jimmy was secretly hoping she wouldn't go and change things, just for the sake of how it looked.

"No more than twenty." Kate stopped and mused. "I always thought of her having a big do."

Jimmy left his boots outside and entered the kitchen barefoot. "Where's my slippers?"

Kate pointed absent mindedly to the corner. "They want to walk, you know."

"Where?"

Kate sounded disappointed. "From the church. They are going to walk down the path, past the school and out to the hall that way,"

Jimmy thought for a moment. "I suppose it makes sense. If they got in a car at the church gates, it's got to go all the way round to the same place."

"Yes" Kate wasn't happy with this, "but what if it's raining, and it means everyone's got to walk as well, unless they all go and get in their little cars and drive round, and that will leave the wedding party------"

"Hang on, hang on." Jimmy had had enough of this but didn't want to dampen her enthusiasm... "You're forgetting something."

"Oh yes, what?" She started to chip the potatoes with a vengeance.

"It's their choice, and it's their wedding, so best go along with it. They've let you take charge of everything else."

"Yes but,--" she stopped as she saw his face. Jimmy was such an easy going carefree sort of person, which is why she fell for him. But his look said "Enough".

Something was making Jenny feel very uneasy. At first she put it down to pre-wedding nerves, but her recent experiences had taught her this was nothing to do with earthly matters.

The only way she could describe it, was that something or someone was trying to get through to her, but her line was busy. Instinct was also telling her not to replace the receiver. She kept these feelings to herself until one evening she and Matthew were sitting in his car overlooking the patchwork of fields which stretched to the far hill. They had been comparing notes on their most recent 'helpers' calling to an earthquake, when her mind flicked to the feelings triggered by the events of her most recent speed travel.

"I know what I meant to tell you," Jenny said. "I had a problem getting back last night, almost as if something was stopping me."

Matthew slowly turned to her. "Why didn't you tell me sooner?"

"We had so much to discuss, and I've only just thought." She was surprised by the dark look that clouded his face, so she added "I'm sure it's nothing, I didn't see anything, I had no image and there was no chill." Then after a moment's silence. "It was something, wasn't it? I can tell by your expression."

Matthew started the car. "I'm not sure. I want to check something." He drove home quicker than Jenny would have liked, but she dare not say anything.

"I'm going to drop you off, I'll see you in a little while. Trust me." He kissed her lightly, hardly waited for her to get out of the car and sped round the corner to Graham's.

"Oh please be in." Matthew glanced at his watch as he waited for the door to be opened. "Eight o'clock. There's still time."

Graham had barely opened the door when Matthew burst in.

"Graham, are you alone?"

"Yes, old chap, what's the matter?"

"Oh thank God you're in. We've got work to do."

Graham beckoned to a chair then sat opposite his friend.

"I think she's being blocked." Matthew ran his fingers through his hair.

"Oh no, don't say that."

Matthew nodded. "She's only had it once, and she won't recognise it."

Graham looked as worried now. "Only one of them, oh no, of course, we won't know will we?"

"Help me find out?"

"Of course. Have you sent for help? We'll need it. They're a powerful, evil lot."

"No time to waste. They could be back tonight, and she travels anywhere these days."

Both settled back in their comfortable chairs and were soon out of body transmitting thoughts ahead as they switched to Eden. The news was not good.

There was a powerful force building on earth which was summoning all kinds of beings, long since banished. The ones from space area Zargon had found a portal through which minor entities were flooding in, creating havoc and unrest. They could block an 'ideal' returning to its earthly form by interfering with the light line, stretching and bending it to make the return difficult. In extreme cases, they had withheld an ideal too long for it to return.

'Ideal' was the general term used by all sources for the other self, the spirit, or soul or any name given to the true being. Previously Graham had pointed out to Jenny that it contained the words Id, idea, I lead, but also a warning reminder in the word 'lied'.

The two men exchanged communication with their principles and agreed the portal must be closed without delay, but where was it? If Jenny was the target of an attempted blocking, maybe it was in their area and if not, how far had the evil spread to reach that point? These were questions that had to be answered and fast.

Matthew asked for guidance on whether Jenny should be informed. He was instructed to make her aware, so as to be on her guard, but not try to take them on. Wasting no time, the two switched to earth and awoke in Graham's sitting room.

"I'm going round to Jenny's." Matthew was already out of his seat.

"Right. I'll get on with trying to find the source."

"Be careful. Wouldn't it be better to wait until we are all together?" Matthew paused at the door.

"I won't go far, just do a bit of probing." Graham waved his friend off and returned to his chair.

Matthew walked quickly round to Jenny's. She was waiting rather impatiently for his return following their earlier conversation, although he had only been gone a few minutes in earth time. He grabbed her hand and said "We must walk."

They were only just out of the cottage when he said "I've found out what is going on, and I'm here to warn you of something very powerful, very evil, deadly in fact."

"Matthew, what is it?" Despite her developments over the months, she began to know fear as she had never felt it before. The images, the fiends were nothing compared with this.

"Let me say at the outset," Matthew stopped in his tracks," the danger from these Zargs, is that you cannot see them, ever."

Jenny's voice was small and strained. "They don't have a form, like you?"

"They are the opposite of us. The bad side. But almost parallel in most other ways. They thought transport, they cannot be seen, and although they can project an image, they rarely do."

"Why is that?"

"No need. They impart such a satanic, malevolent feeling, that an image is almost unnecessary.

Jenny shuddered at the thought. "And you think this is what was blocking my return. I saw nothing and I can't say I felt any evil."

"You wouldn't, not at first. They were trying you out. Finding how powerful you are."

"Oh Matthew, just before our wedding. They won't spoil it will they?"

"That's what Graham and I have to ensure."

"What do you mean? What about me?"

"Jenny" he pulled her to him. "I only warned you for you to be on your guard. You're not ready to fight these yet."

"But --"

"No." He was firm. "We know what we are up against, and believe me, it's not for beginners."

"So how am I supposed to learn, gain experience?"

"You will, in good time, but this isn't the time." He turned her round and they headed back to the cottage.

"What about thought travel?" An idea struck Jenny. "I was in speed mode, wouldn't that make a difference?"

"Thought travel makes it slightly more difficult" he said slowly, but don't forget they can do it too. AND you are still connected through the line, or you couldn't return."

"Even in thought." she mused to herself.

"Even in thought "he reiterated.

As they reached the gate he said softly "Promise me you won't travel far tonight my little elfin."

"Oh Matthew, I promised Marie, I can't let her down."

"Alright, but be careful." They kissed for several minutes before he left for the task which made even him shudder.

Chapter 14

"I really appreciate your coming, in the circumstances." Marie's warmth touched Jenny as they hovered over a makeshift hospital at the aftermath of an earthquake. The news had been transmitted to her and all helpers immediately.

"Makes you wonder if they had anything to do with this." Jenny directed her thoughts to the carnage below.

"Oh, they'd enjoy it."

The two friends moved together looking for their next allocated ideal as Marie said "Better stay close." Jenny nodded in agreement and indicated to a little boy whose body had been stripped of its legs and half an arm. As his ideal rose, Marie said "Yours I think, you have a way with the little ones."

"Mummy" the thought rose with him as Jenny enveloped him in her arms.

"I know darling, you'll be alright now." As he looked past her she saw Marie comforting a young woman.

"My baby, where's my baby?" Realisation hit Jenny as the mother saw the boy and rushed to embrace him.

"Can we leave them together?" Jenny was full of emotion and felt like an intruder.

"Not yet." Marie moved close to Jenny. "Don't forget, they need us to help them through transition. They are vulnerable."

"Yes. The Zargs."

"Not only them." Marie started to move back to the mother and child. "There are many lesser ones who, although not so evil, will have their wicked way, if we let them."

There was much to do, but suddenly Marie indicated for Jenny to return to her bodily form.

"Matthew and Graham are waiting to see you safely in. Go now." They exchanged farewells and Marie went back to her work.

"I'll use thought," Jenny switched, and was gone.

She should have immediately awoken in her body, but instead felt herself held at a distance, her light line stretched as though it would snap. She tried to get her bearings as she had no idea of how far she had travelled in thought. Distance was no factor in this mode. Whether it be an earth location, as this had been, or from Eden, or even when Marie took her to Saturn, the instant thought would transport her ideal in a flash.

There was a city below her, so she descended slowly trying to identify with a familiar landmark, her line still taut. It was Oxford, so she was about twenty miles from home. She decided to travel the line slowly until she knew what was controlling it so she rose up and tried to go forward. Not at her own will but by an unseen force she was moved away from the city lights until she was hovering in darkness, held by a powerful hand, unable to go in any direction. In desperation, she tried to summon her colours and sound although this seemed rather basic for the force which held her in its grasp.

Suddenly she went forward with a jerk, as though she had found a weakness, then again she was held as though the power had regained its hold. Her brain was racing for a way to outwit this new foe but she was aware it would be one step ahead. She relaxed everything, her hold, her fight and her mind. Then in an instant directed all her power into a projection of a piercing high pitched whine accompanied, not by beautiful colour, but a powerful highly charged bolt of lightning. Even the force which had held her up until that moment could not have envisaged what followed.

Every race, every being from all space areas fought the evil of the Zargs. All had felt the terror at some time, and singly could do little, but forces were gathering.

Attracted by Jenny's sudden electrical impulse, a group of Schynings diverted to help her, calling others to them. Some were delivering, some collecting, it didn't matter. They didn't have to see anything in form or image, they knew from experience just what evil she was fighting.

Guiding their light panels and spheres into a concentrated group above her, they directed enough electrical power to fry anything in their path. Then silently shot away before Jenny could offer thanks. She realised she was free to move and travelled slowly, cautiously down her now flexible line to her body.

Matthew and Graham were just above her home anxiously awaiting her arrival. "You are alright." Her fiancé almost shouted, "we feared the worst."

Graham added, "We were guarding your return, but they must have gone out to waylay you."

"I'm OK, I had help." And she related the events in an instant of thought before safely returning to her bed.

For once it was Jimmy who had gone to his daughter's bedroom in the early hours. He watched as she lay there, eyes wide, her mouth open in a scream which did not come. She gave a sudden jolt, closed her eyes and mouth, turned over and continued to sleep.

"Best not worry Kate" he thought. "The girl's alright."

"What time is it?" His return to bed had woken her.

"About half past four, I think. She's alright, I've just been in."

The local papers were soon full of pictures of the tree that had been struck by lightning on the Charlbury road. Speculative reports tried to hazard a guess at how it had happened. There had been no storm, as far as anybody knew, although somebody thought they saw a flash of light in the distance, as they were going to work in the early morning. Further afield there were reports of strange lights which hovered together, then sped away at great speed but with no sound. Kate read the evening edition and slowly put down the paper.

"Jimmy."

He turned down the television knowing the tone in her voice. "Yes."

"You've read it?"

"I've read it."

"What do you make of it?"

"I don't know."

Kate tutted. "It must have been about the same time."

"She was alright this morning." Jimmy went to turn the television back up.

"Was she? She looked drained to me. There's more to this than I can fathom."

Knowing she wasn't going to get any more response from her husband, she reluctantly settled back to watch the programme.

Something made Jenny's ears prick up. Tony, a local lad had popped into her place of work to deliver something for her boss.

"Had any good séances lately Mrs.?" His lighthearted question was directed at Mrs. Randle, but Jenny was quick to notice the reaction of the woman.

"Why, what is it to you?" she snapped at him.

"Only asked, keep your hair on love." He shrugged at Jenny, and with a whistle he was off.

"Now, that's not like you Mrs. R." Jenny felt in full command of the situation. "You normally want to share your sessions with all of us."

Mrs. Randle seemed to crumble and Jenny thought she was going to burst into tears.

"What on earth's the matter?" This was no play acting. The older woman was clearly distressed.

"Tell you later." she sniffed into a hanky.

At lunchtime, Jenny made them both a cup of tea and sat down opposite Mrs. R.

"Now then," she started, "tell me all about it."

"It was at the weekend, Sunday actually. We were having a meeting."

"Do you mean a séance?" Jenny looked straight at her.

"Well, yes, you could call it that. Yes it was. I've known these people for a long time, and now and again, we get together you see."

"She's being evasive," thought Jenny, "she doesn't want to tell me because she's got something to hide." Aloud "Go on."

"Well, there's this foreign gentleman, he comes through quite often, he's like a guardian, and he was trying to warn me."

"Oh yes. What about?"

"Danger. He said I didn't know what I was doing."

"Probably right." Jenny didn't voice her opinion.

"But then, the room filled with a horrible smell, like something rotting, and there was this awful feeling of evil. I tried to get rid of it, to banish it from the room, but it wouldn't go." She was sobbing, with perspiration running down her face.

Jenny put an arm round to comfort her. "Where do you live, exactly Mrs. Randle?"

"Hook Norton." She gave a brief description of where her house was situated.

"Why. What do you want to know for?"

"Never mind for now. Is that all?"

"Well, we put the lights on, we were all very shaken you understand, and then-- and then ---" she started to cry again. "My friend's husband Tom became ill and was very sick." She looked up at Jenny. "It's all my fault."

"Well we don't know about that, but best give it a rest for a while, eh?"

Mrs. Randle nodded, blew her nose loudly and tried to compose herself.

Jenny phoned Matthew at the first opportunity. No good relying on thought at this time of day, the physical method would be more effective.

"I think I've found a portal, although there may be others."

"Good girl," his elation came down the phone line. "Where?"

Mrs. Randle."

"Of course, I should have thought of that, but the trouble is we never give the dabblers much credence. Although they cause more trouble."

They agreed to meet with Graham to discuss this new found valuable information. Jenny mulled it over in her brain. If there was a portal at Mrs. Randle's, that is why she had been such an easy target. Her mind turned back to her imminent marriage. Mr. and Mrs. Randle had been invited as guests.

"Oh I do hope she leaves all her connections behind." Jenny was a little amused by the prospect, but soon the gravity of it sobered her as she recalled her recent struggle to return.

"Little does she know what she has unleashed." She felt a surge of anger. "Why must people play with what they don't understand?"

Chapter 15

In spite of the impending battle against the evil forces, Jenny's mind still demanded the answers to many questions. Since the helping hand extended by the Schynings, it made her ask why, with so many cosmic sources, did the aliens all look like earth people.

"But they don't," Matthew explained. "Remember the American situation, with the French, the Spanish, etc?"

"Yes, but they all look the same."

"Matthew screwed up his face."Do they really? Are you sure about that?"

Jenny knew there was a hidden meaning in such a simple question.

"Well, I suppose the Spanish have a certain look, and Orientals have different eyes and yellowier skin. Many of the Indian races, and the pygmies are small. And then there are the other dark skinned in many tones."

"I think you have answered your own enquiry, don't you?"

"But are you saying, each race is not only situated on a different part of earth, they all came from their individual sources?"

"I am indeed. But they aren't so split any more are they. In many cities, there are dozens of different ethnic groups living alongside. But they accept it, because nobody has ever questioned it."

"I thought the dark skinned had evolved like that because of the amount of sun in their part of the world." Jenny thought she had found a little loophole.

"So it has been believed because nobody knew any different. The truth is, their space area is much nearer the sun which is what caused the pigmentation."

"But they must have arrived sometime, didn't anybody query it then?"

"Why should they?" Matthew was being patient. He knew this was a lot to absorb. Like most people, he was asking Jenny to change her thinking which had been with her all her life. The thought snapped "But she isn't 'most people'.

"Look at it this way. They arrive, say in Africa. Live there for centuries undisturbed until some clever explorer realises there are other bits of land on this chunk of rock. And he goes and discovers them, and what does everybody assume?"

"That they've been there all the time." Jenny nodded in agreement. "When you stop and work it out, it's quite logical, isn't it?"

"It's the truth."

It was two days before the wedding. Everything that could be done, with the exception of the inevitable last minute bits, had been done. Jenny had taken a couple of days off work for several reasons. She wanted to make sure her mother didn't run herself completely into the ground, and she wanted time to relax and travel at will knowing the unseen problem that was loiterng, waiting for an unguarded moment to pounce.

They were sharing a quiet cup of tea after having put the finishing touches to Jenny's going away outfit.

"So, you still haven't said just where it is you are going on your honeymoon." Kate was determined to prise it out of her.

Jenny answered with a laugh. "Mother dear, you know very well that is a secret from everyone, but if it will make you any happier, I will ring you at least once."

"It will be strange." Kate's lower lip quivered." Not to have you around any more. Barely nineteen, and leaving home."

"We've been through this, I'm not leaving home as such, I am getting married to a wonderful man, and naturally I will live with him, not here." Jenny was being very precise as she felt her mother was turning on the guilt tactics. She had already been through the "It won't be the same anymore" bit and the "The first birthday you've ever been away from home" bit, so she was getting steeled to the daily little arrows that were being fired.

"A few years ago," Kate tried a different approach, "I would have sworn you would never leave home, never find anybody."

"Wow," Jenny thought, "she's trying to get back to that one again."

"I don't care what anybody says----"Kate began.

"More tea?" Jenny tried to cut the stream of self pity.

"No thank you, like I was saying, you are a different girl now," she paused expecting a reply. Jenny eyed her in silence forcing Kate to continue. "To what you were." Again she waited for Jenny's reply. She did not expect the reaction that followed.

"Mother, you know I love you dearly, and I am grateful for all you have done for this wedding, but please be certain of one thing." Her face had paled, her eyes piercing and her mouth set. The words were clipped and almost spat out.

"I am NOT your little girl. I am a self assured young woman. You think you know me but you know nothing. It is time to break the ties, to let me go. You are happy in your sweet contented little world, where the main event of your day is if a bird drops its load on your washing. Well listen to me, there is more out there than you could ever imagine, and I am part of it."

Jenny's face was so distorted, Kate visibly trembled at the sight of it. She had witnessed the changes that happened when the girl was asleep, but she had never seen anything so horrible during the waking hours. It was too much for her to bear, and she broke down and sobbed. Jenny shook herself, hardly sure of what had taken her over, although she had a good idea. No image, no chill, but a force that could, in an instant, turn her against the woman who had carried her and loved her with such an innocent affection, who gave all and expected nothing in return.

She flew to her mother, embraced her and cried with her. The terrified creature in her arms tried to struggle free.

"Mother, it's me. That wasn't me. Believe me."

Kate was still shaking. "I know that. But that's what I've been trying to tell you. I know it isn't you, but what is it?"

"I don't know Mother, but whatever it is, I want to keep it away from you. Don't you see, that's partly why I'm going to live near Woodstock. To leave you in peace."

"Was it, - um - did it start when you met Matthew? I have to know."

Jenny held her mother's hand in both of hers. "Not really. It was always there somewhere. But don't ask me too much."

"But I worry about you."

"Yes I know you do, and I love you for it you sweet thing. Now, should we do something about getting a meal?"

Kate had to resign herself to the meagre scrap of information. It didn't really make her feel any better, it just fuelled her worries now she believed there was something possessing her daughter, although she had no idea what.

That evening, Jenny popped round to Graham's. Matthew was already there and the three settled down to update each other on any recent events.

"I flew at Mum today," Jenny still felt guilty, "only I think there was more too it. I think my appearance changed, by the look she gave me, but I couldn't ask."

"What time was this?" Graham leaned forward. "Was it by any chance around four o'clock?"

"Yes it was, we were having a cup of tea. How did you know?"

Matthew and Graham exchanged glances. "We were in walking travel, and we intercepted a Zarg. At least we feel we did." Graham looked towards his friend for support.

Matthew said slowly. "We were at Mrs. Randle's."

Jenny looked from one to the other. "Oh no."

Matthew nodded. "There IS a portal there. The silly woman's opened it, she probably didn't even realise it."

"Is it still open? Couldn't you close it?"

Graham cut in "It isn't that simple. It isn't just a door."

Matthew saw Jenny's face and said "Gently old boy, she hasn't encountered anything like this. We have."

"Sorry Jen," Graham patted her arm.

"No, it's alright, I realise I'm new to it. Go on."

Matthew stood up and paced for a moment. "Shall I try and explain?"

Graham nodded.

"OK." Matthew sat down next to Jenny. "There are many forces just waiting around for a niche where they can enter a world, it doesn't have to be this one, and cause disasters, illness, plague, famine, in fact every terrible crisis you can name."

Jenny's mouth dropped. "You mean they don't just happen."

"Well some do, but not on the scale we are talking about. They are caused."

"But what about the good forces? Don't they fight them?"

Graham smiled. "We try to."

"You see, time is no object to them" Matthew continued, "after all what is time?"

Graham added his point. "There is no end to time, so there is never any hurry. They wait for any opportunity."

"Which is why you have always drummed it into me to be on my guard."

"Exactly." The two men spoke together. Matthew cast a glance at his watch and said hurriedly "We must push on. Everything has a surrounding protective field."

"Is that what some people call an aura?" Jenny had seen drawings of these.

"To a degree." Matthew should have expected that and he smiled. "You've used yours a few times. But take the three of us. Combined, imagine the force field power we can generate."

Again Graham wanted to contribute. "Combined energy Jenny. That is why the Schynings often travel together, especially if danger threatens."

"Does it really work?" Jenny could understand it so far.

Matthew squeezed her hand. "Of course. But back to the portal. If you get areas of weak power, it doesn't take much for a powerful force to push its way through, even if there isn't an obvious break. Now, if you get a meddler, like Mrs. Randle, who may have enough power to connect to something awaiting the call, it's not going to refuse an opening offered on a plate, is it?"

Jenny was staring wide eyed. "As simple as that?"

"He makes it sound simple," Graham smiled."Which is why he is so good at his job."

Matthew was stern as he said "Jokes have been made about 'Is there anybody there?' well you bet there is. There isn't only one portal. They are all over space with little sentries guarding them. Waiting. Can you imagine what happens the moment one gains entry?"

After a pause Jenny ventured "They send messages back."

"Like a grapevine." Matthew confirmed.

"And," Jenny was trying to remember everything she had been taught, "they can thought travel like us, so "she stopped for a moment as she tried to mentally sort the facts, "they don't actually walk in, they are here in thought immediately."

Graham looked quizzical." Not all. The Zargs can, but the lesser entities have to be, how shall I put it, escorted."

Jenny looked from one to the other. "That is why it is so difficult to trace them, with some having no form etc."

"You've got it." Matthew said.

"So what do you do?"

Matthew let out a big sigh. "I'm afraid it is the never ending battle between good and bad. We banish as many as we can, close the portals for now and good has won for the time being. Then we get a situation like this, when floods of them get in and off we go again."

"But," Jenny's mind was reaching beyond earth, "you say it happens all over space?"

"Inevitable. Every galaxy I expect. I don't think anyone would know how to cope with perfect existence."

Jenny smiled a little. "What beats me, is that most people go about their everyday lives, oblivious of all this."

"Ah," Graham cut in "as far as you know. Unless you meet walkers, or helpers, or people in speed that you recognise, how do you know who is who?"

"Same with the entities," Matthew reminded her. "You can't always sort the good from the bad. They don't go around with a sign over themselves"

"Bit like human beings." Jenny laughed.

Matthew clapped his hands briefly. "Let's not forget why we are here. Jenny, we have work to do. Do you feel up to it?"

"Of course I do. Why ask?"

"We were thinking of the wedding" Graham said. "We don't want you in danger."

"Tell me what to do." She turned to Matthew "We may as well start sharing everything now." So the three made their plans for the approaching night.

Chapter 16

Mrs. Randle could hardly bear to enter her front room. Ever since the séance it held a chill never before known to her. Although help was at hand, the poor creature didn't realise it. Had she been as experienced in the occult as she would have liked, the trio rapidly approaching could have worked with her, whereas she would have no knowledge whatsoever of the turmoil which was to take place on her premises.

Matthew and Graham flanked Jenny for support and protection. Before retiring for the night they had washed several times from head to toe and put on clean nightwear. Every minute detail had to be as sterile as possible, their bodies, clothing and even their minds. They travelled in the appropriate garb of long white gowns with white close fitting caps. They purposely emptied their minds of all the junk, and concentrated on their love for each other and a strong revulsion of all things evil.

As they approached Mrs Randle's house, they were met by eight others in like apparel. Nothing was exchanged apart from a slight acknowledgment of each other's presence. Matthew was obviously in charge as he was the most experienced in such events, and he beckoned them all into the front room where they formed a circle with a space opposite his own position.

The atmosphere was horrific. The place positively reeked of evil, its nucleus centred in a spot just above the table. Jenny hadn't really known what to expect, but somehow had imagined a flat area, like a door, with a slit in it. The spiral tornado of an opening could be clearly seen and, although directing upwards, gave off the impression of being the entrance to Hell.

All eleven ideals were circled round this centre of turmoil.

"I wonder why we are waiting." Jenny dare not pass this thought. "And who will be the twelfth to fill the gap?"

As if in answer, the room was filled with light and a form slowly appeared opposite Matthew. The circle was complete. Jenny was carried along with the procedure, although it seemed to come as second nature to her, and it was only later she marvelled at her reactions.

The ideals, now being in position, started squeezing together until it felt as though they merged into one almighty powerful force. The intense pressure they expelled was squeezing the portal into a narrower gap until the base was nothing more than a hair's breadth. They continued, exerting more power as their combined efforts seemed to fuel the point where the twelfth had positioned. The portal was being squeezed slowly up from the bottom until it reached the ceiling. The circle continued the power for this was only the beginning. It had to lift the opening high enough, away from the earth's gravity, and far out into space.

As the Powerful One on Eden observed the operation, he saw the vortex lift, and as it reached his level, he gave it his own push, sending it hurtling to another galaxy.

"Well done my children." was his thought as he awaited the return of his son.

The pressure extinguished, the twelve slowly separated, their heads lowered. Eleven stayed in the same position, as the twelfth gently touched their crowns sending a beautiful feeling of peace through them. When they all raised their eyes simultaneously, there were only eleven, with a space opposite Matthew.

The room was still. The warmth was gradually creeping back in as the door opened. Mrs. Randle looked about her, seeing only her familiar surroundings. She sat at the table, put her head in her hands and cried.

"I don't know who you are, but praise be to you."

Matthew ushered the group outside." I think we will let her have her home back now." He thanked the eight, who quickly bid the three friends farewell and switched away to their own forms.

"Well, that has stemmed the tide of this lot." Graham felt the task was completed and was a little surprised when it was Jenny who said "I don't think we should be too complacent yet."

Both men turned to her. She looked towards the direction of their home.

"We have not returned." Her thought message was clear and direct as though she had assumed control.

Matthew was quick to notice this and said "She's right. We don't want anything going wrong now."

"The Zargs won't be too pleased." Graham saw the sense of it. "Closing their little opening for their supporters."

Jenny positioned herself slightly in front of the men. "Time to go."

Matthew took command. "Thought travel everyone, it's safer. Switch now."

All three light lines had been tangled, making it difficult for the three to go directly home. Fortunately, Matthew had had the foresight to station helper guards at the return point, as he guessed something like this would be actioned. Although the volunteers had not been able to clear the paths completely, the friends did not meet the obstacles which had been planned.

Back in her bed Jenny lay thinking. Only one more day to go, and she would be Mrs. Matthew Gavrielle. She prayed that nothing in this world, or any other, would hamper the fruition of this dream. But she had found a new strength. No longer did she shrink from those aggravating little forces which once played with her. She was growing in power and she knew it.

"They still haven't told me who I am and where I came from." The idea hit her like a bolt. But with the wedding so near she resigned herself to giving all her attention to her big day. Then, she would demand to know. And she would be told.

Much to everyone's relief, Saturday dawned dry but with a slight chilly breeze. Kate assured everyone it would warm up by the wedding time of two o'clock. Matthew had decided to stay at Graham's as it was on the doorstep, with a strict promise to stay out of sight, so that he and his future bride would have no chance of meeting before the ceremony. Aunt Doris and Anne arrived in good time for Kate to fuss over Anne's dress, but she needn't have worried for it fitted perfectly without any adjustments needed. Kate herself looked, as Jenny had predicted, absolutely stunning and Jimmy in his new suit looked almost handsome, in a rugged sort of way. Jenny appeared in her dress and veil and almost floated down the stairs. The ladies all had a pretend little weep, although Kate's was more nearer the real thing than she cared to admit. Anne handed the bride her bouquet made up of white rose buds with tiny traces of blue ribbon dotted through. This had been a special request from Jenny. She recalled something she had said to Matthew, and it seemed important to have it represented on her special day. White noise is heavenly blue.

Matthew and his best man, Graham looked immaculate in their matching pale grey suits. Their buttonholes were white carnations bound with blue ribbon. It was obvious to all that the groom's parents were used to 'dressing up' as Jimmy put it. Ma's outfit was designer label for sure, her hat must have cost more than the whole bride's side put together, and Pa's had never seen a peg, let alone come off one. But being used to it, they carried the effect well, were not at all stuffy, and seemed to enjoy the day as much as anyone.

Jimmy whispered to Kate at one point, "Does 'em good to rough it once in a while" for which he received one of his wife's "Behave yourself" looks.

Everything went according to plan, even the walk from the church to the reception, which had been worrying Kate, took on a very relaxed peaceful atmosphere, and seemed to be to the enjoyment of all.

The two tiered cake, trimmed with tiny blue flowers, was a work of art and very much in keeping with the colour scheme. After the usual speeches, toasting, reading of cards and general chatting with the guests, the newly weds left to change for their honeymoon.

Matthew's car had been locked away to avoid any trimming up, much to Jenny's delight. She didn't want to announce to everyone they were just married. Instead she wanted her beloved all to herself, to quietly enjoy some earthly pleasure at last and surrender her pent up physical desires to her husband, for she was now Mrs. Matthew Gavrielle, his wife.

They arrived at their honeymoon hotel fairly late that evening, and being rather tired, went straight to bed. As he held her in his arms in their shared love nest, Matthew too wanted to shut out the world, the forces which he knew they would continue to fight, and anything that could possibly separate him from his love. An annoying ache warned him of the impending pressure he knew would try to tear them apart, and he prayed to the Powerful One not to let it happen.

He made love to her, gently at first, knowing she was untouched and as pure as the blooms she had carried. Her ideal was already showing signs of battle scars, but he thought to himself as he exploded into her "I'm not making love to her ideal. I am giving myself to my wife. "They merged in love as one being, this time to join themselves in affection, not to rid the world of evil forces.

They toured the south coast for a week, visiting many places and it would have been easy to pretend that was the extent of their domain, but at night both knew better, and they continued to travel, although with great caution.

On their return, they moved into part of Matthew's parent's house. Kate had not hidden her surprise when they told her, feeling they should look for a place of their own. Mr. and Mrs. Gavrielle senior were off again to their villa in Spain and really did not need such a large property all to themselves, and having always had the idea that Matthew would inherit it someday, it seemed ideal for him to remain in situ. There was plenty of room for them all to live under the same roof whenever they returned, and still be self contained.

Jenny was going to look for another job at an estate agents in Woodstock, as she felt it would be too far to go to Chipping Norton every day. Matthew didn't really want her to work, but as he was often away all day, gave in because he knew she would rather keep herself active. They compromised with the idea of her only working part time thus giving her plenty of opportunity to visit her parents whenever the need arose. She intended to learn to drive, something she had been meaning to do for some time, and this would mean she didn't have to rely on buses and would give her more freedom.

As they settled into their new existence, the old burning question rose to the surface demanding immediate attention.

Where was Jenny's space area? And what was her true identity? Circumstances dictated she was about to find out.

Chapter 17

The newly weds had been home a week, when Matthew said, "Somethings's not right."

They were relaxing in the garden on a lazy Sunday afternoon casually exchanging the odd word. The warmth was lulling Jenny almost to sleep, but something in her husband's voice made her sit up.

"Such as?" She turned to look at him.

"It's too quiet." He looked very serious and Jenny knew he would not speak without cause.

"I take it you aren't talking physically?" she looked around the garden with the birds singing and the flowers dancing in the spasmodic breezes.

"No. Since the portal closing, the Zargs have gone inactive. That's not like them unless they are planning something big."

Jenny too was serious now. "I thought we had been lucky, but you said we were getting extra protection around our marriage, and I thought that was it."

Matthew shook his head. "No, the helpers only stayed for a couple of days over the ceremony time to help protect us, let us relax a little, but they were called away."

"Oh yes," Jenny recalled "they have more important things to do, but I did appreciate them."

Matthew was deep in thought. "I expected some activity when we travelled, especially by now. But you can sense it can't you? I wish I knew what it was. Even the greater powers on Eden don't know, which is unusual. I tell you my love, it's something enormous."

They were interrupted by the telephone ringing. Matthew picked up the handset on the little garden table between them. The caller must have spoken immediately for there was no exchange of salutation, instead Matthew answered straight into the conversation.

"Oh no. Don't say that." He was visibly moved. "Ok thanks Graham."

He replaced the phone in silence.

"What is it?" Jenny's voice was barely heard.

"Now I know." Matthew covered his face for a moment. Then looking at her he said quietly "HE's back. So that's what it's all about."

"You don't mean----" her voice trailed off.

"I do mean. Zargot. What's he doing here? He doesn't visit himself, he leaves it to his underlings, and they're bad enough."

Jenny's voice shook and she reached for Matthew's hand for support.

"There is a focus isn't there? There's somebody in particular they are aiming for?"

"Oh Jenny, my love" He moved to her side and held her so close she could hardly breathe. "Ready or not, you are going to have to know the full details."

"About me?" she knew the answer already.

"Yes my darling, very much about you."

Kate was adjusting to life without her little girl. She went about her tasks like a martyr. "Don't mind me, I'll be alright." She repeated this so many times, Jimmy was almost saying it with her.

"I've told you," he would try to let her see he understood, "she's fallen on her feet. She'll not want for anything and the lad loves her. Why can't you just be glad she's found a good'un?"

"If only you knew" she thought to herself remembering the outburst prior to the wedding.

"Anyway, she'll be coming over to see you soon. She's not got a new job yet, so you two can do things women do."

"I suppose you're right, as usual." She planted a kiss on his forehead, grateful that he was a 'down to earth' normal sort of a fellow.

"Which is more than he is" she thought, her mind turning to Matthew.

Matthew had moved the sun loungers close together so that he could hold Jenny close while he poured out the most illuminating information of her training.

"You have no recollection at all of your source do you?"

Jenny looked far away. "Well, sometimes, I almost feel as though----- I don't know how to describe it, sort of as if I had lost my memory and now and again something triggers a vague glimpse of--" her voice trailed off. "It's there, and yet it isn't. Am I making sense?"

Matthew took a deep breath. "I had better tell you the full story. Try and take it in but it won't be easy to digest."

She nodded in agreement and settled herself comfortably.

Matthew coughed nervously.

"Right. For a start you don't think you are from Eden because you don't have total recall of any previous life. That could be because this is your first visit on this planet, but that isn't the case. Not only are you from Eden, " he hesitated "but you are the daughter of the Powerful One, The Almighty Being who is the Principal of all goodness, anywhere." He let the words sink in before continuing. Jenny sat with her mouth open. Matthew, having got over the worst bit continued.

"You were a force to be reckoned with. You brought terror to the evil ones. No-one could crush them like you. Your father was so proud of you, you did your job and you did it to perfection. When I think of the times you rid an area of evil ones, including the Zargs, you almost swept Schyn clean of them. Why do you think they rushed to help you?"

Jenny had paled considerably.

"Matthew?"

"Yes my dearest."

"You keep using the past tense. What happened?"

He stroked her hand gently.

"You have inhabited many space areas, in fact most in this galaxy, Your six lives on Saturn were your favourite and you have always had a soft spot for that planet."

"Yes, Marie takes me there sometimes even now." Jenny smiled at the peaceful feeling the place exuded...

"To get back to the main theme." Matthew could easily have veered away from the task in front of him. "You had completed six of your seven earth lives and were due to be repositioned for the final one. There had been a general overpowering of the Zargs and their sadistic leader, Zargot had come to put the records straight. He was here for revenge in a big way. During your waiting period, between six and seven, you did a magnificent job of overpowering him with such cunning, the whole universe reeled in admiration for you." Matthew paused to take a sip from his drink. Jenny was so overcome at what was enfolding, that for once she was silent.

"It went very quiet, much like it is now."

Jenny found her voice. "That is why you are so worried."

He nodded. “It came time for you to be placed into your seventh life, and that is when Zargot and his followers struck. They intercepted the carriers, overpowered them and attempted to despatch you as far away as possible."

"Oh no." Jenny's stomach churned. She wasn't sure if she really wanted to hear any more, but curiosity got the better of her.

"Are you OK for me to continue." Matthew felt he wasn't making a good job of this.

"I'm fine, please, continue."

"As soon as your father realised you had not been re-positioned, he sent his most powerful amongst us to trace you. Zargot only got as far as Jupiter before he was intercepted." He paused, very distressed at what was to come. Now it was Jenny's turn to comfort him.

"Don't, not if you don't want to." They were both crying together.

"No. I have to do it." He composed himself. "Zargot propelled you towards the red spot, the gigantic storm. We couldn't get you out. You couldn't thought travel." The words were coming out stilted as he relived the horrific moment.

"You couldn't have existed, had you been given life, but it was your time for re-positioning. Do you understand what I am saying?" He was almost hysterical.

"I- I -m not sure. Did I have to stay there? I have a feeling I was trapped in the storm."

"You were my darling, you were. Your soul mate was uncontrollable, he insisted on going with us. It took all our power to hold him back"

"My soul mate?" Jenny had never heard Matthew speak of a soul mate before. Why was that?

"It wasn't you was it?" She knew the reply. He shook his head.

"No. It wasn't me." He kissed her knowing this was the moment he had been dreading. Fortunately she didn't pursue it for now.

"How long was I in there, and how did I get out?" This was the next obvious point of the story to her.

"You were in there long enough for your entire memory, that is your ideal's memory to be erased. At least we hope it is only a temporary erasure. The signs are good at the moment. You have grown in experience and power so dramatically that we are all hopeful."

"And?" She was still very quiet, although she was absorbing it all up to now.

"You got out, because you could not exist in there. In simple terms, you died."

"But I hadn't been born."

"Yes you had, in some sort of particle, who knows. You were given a life of some sort. A life on Jupiter and when it was over, we were waiting to take your ideal back. Your soul mate transported you, or what was left." His voice trailed off.

There was a long silence while the awful truth began to sink into Jenny's mind.

"I'm having to learn everything all over again, aren't I? That's why you were sent wasn't it, to teach me?

"Now that's more like it, I can cope with you firing questions at me." He gave her a squeeze. "When it was considered fitting, we had to let you undergo your seventh life as planned. Only this time it was like a military operation. We selected perfect parents who would let you grow up in quiet surroundings, not pestering you, until we were ready to move in."

Jenny smiled a little now. "The colours and white noise."

"Is it making sense?" He was glad she hadn't gone to pieces, but he couldn't have blamed her.

"Yes, it is, but when you took me to Eden, why didn't I meet my father?"

"It wasn't the right time. But he saw you and was very pleased with your progress, but back to Zargot. Now do you see why this is serious?"

Jenny answered with another question. "It's me he's after isn't it?"

"Well, he did loose face, thanks to you. He won't let that go, until he's settled the score."

Jenny looked puzzled. "Wait a minute. If I can't remember, if I haven't regained my power, what chance to I have?"

"Ah. He doesn't know that, we are sure of it. That's why his little sentinels have been checking you out. I think some have already had a few nasty surprises from you."

She had to smile at that. "You could say I gave them more than they bargained for." This lightened the mood considerably. But it changed just as quickly as she said "How did Graham know Zargot was back?"

"News travels fast between the Powerful One's top notch powers."

"Of which you are one. So Graham is as well?"

"He is."

"Have you both done your seven?"

Matthew looked almost superior. "This is my seventh. Graham is on his sixth, although he is so advanced, his seventh will be brief. He will be born but die almost immediately."

She looked sad for a moment, but then remembered her Jupiter life.

"You said my soul mate took me back to Eden. Would I know him?"

This was the moment of truth for Matthew.

"Ye-s " he almost stretched the word. "You would, you do know him."

"But who?"

Matthew did no more than pick up the telephone and show it to his wife.

"Graham!"

He put it down, got up and went into the house before Jenny could see the tears streaming down his face.

Chapter 18

On the planet earth there are many large plains, deserts, and places which are rarely visited by man, thus affording perfect hiding places for mustering forces. One such desert now served this purpose for Zargot and his people. Unseen, they were building up the largest evil power ever known. His sentinels guarded every possible portal to drag in any race or entity that was either evil already, or too afraid of the consequences to object. So his power thrived on more power

When Matthew had explained to Jenny about the Zargs not needing a form, he did not tell her that some were positioned in human babies, to grow and be at hand in earthly form when required. Some of these creatures had been working at a desert base for many years, undetected by military forces. What they were doing was so despicable, but typical of their kind.

They wanted to produce a living form that could travel the universe but not have the need for suspended animation. They would be living computers. There would be little use for the body except for pushing buttons on command so that was bred into a thin spindly shape. The head had to be large to accommodate the oversized brain, the eyes able to cope with intense light and heat, and the tiny nose and mouth only for use in communication. They would not need to eat or drink and therefore would produce no waste. Power would be from an electrical source, the sun whenever possible. Colour had to be non descript and the final result was a pale silvery grey.

The horrible side effect lay in the failures along the path of perfection. Many terribly deformed creatures were produced as the Zargs experimented. Some were poisoned, but the sadistic creatures who had given them life, refused to spare them all from further suffering, and used them for observations.

The factor which overshadowed even this cruelty, was how they bred them in the first place.

There have, for many years, been reports of alien abduction, the description of the beings similar to the hybrids being turned out at the desert base. They would overcome a human, usually female, by thought power, and extract some of her eggs. These would be stored until fertilised by the seed from the bodies inhabited by the Zargs, then mutilated and adapted until the required format was achieved.

They used their technique of time bending to add to the confusion, so the abductees' stories that eventually emerged held an element of doubt. The beings could wipe a brain pattern so that, although the prisoner thought they had been taken for a few minutes, they would be returned several earth hours later. Alternatively, if they felt they had been kept for many hours, even days, they would return to find only a few minutes had elapsed.

These were the species Zargot had specially designed to travel in physical form, if the living hell could take on such a description. This was his way of controlling, not only the universe, but each individual planet on a physical basis. In other words, he would become the ultimate ruler of all things.

Matthew washed his face, forced a smile and rejoined his wife, still recoiling from his last narration.

She smiled and held up her hand as he sat beside her. "Don't be cross," she said, "but I've just phoned Graham"

Matthew started to speak but she put her hand to his lips and continued. "I've told him I know. I have also told him, that although he may be my soul mate, I am married to you, I'm deeply in love with you, and things will remain that way."

"You told him that!" Matthew was shocked.

"I certainly did. You didn't think I wouldn't want you any more did you?"

"It's something I've been dreading, you finding out. That's why I put it off so long." He hugged her.

"You silly." she laughed aloud but then said "Poor Graham, he must have been through hell. Still is, only he doesn't show it. "

"He will have you after this life though." Matthew saddened at the thought.

"And so will you. You don't think I'd desert you do you? All three of us can be together. Oh wait a minute. Haven't we forgotten something?"

"What?"

"Don't you have a soul mate?"

"No."

"But I thought everybody had one." She was amazed.

"Now whoever said it was compulsory?" He gave her one of his enquiring looks, his head on one side.

"No-one I suppose, I just thought."

"Biggest mistake people make." He settled back on his lounger. "Are you ready for any more yet, or have you had enough?"

"No. Tell me all you can. I think it could be triggering, and the more I can remember, the less vulnerable I feel.

Although a weight had been lifted from Matthew's heart, another one replaced it just as quickly. When his work was done and Jenny was restored to full power, he would be recalled.

"But no sooner than is necessary" he thought.

Mrs. Randle soon got over her unpleasant experience, as she called it, and like so many dabblers, never learned by her mistakes. Her friends from the the last séance had ignored her and she felt lonely. but she was the kind of person who always had to have an audience, and her meetings provided one. At this point she decided to put an advertisement in the local paper. There were always people who needed to contact loved ones, and there was the money she would charge. Carefully placing the entry under a box number, she sat back to await her replies. She also thought about giving Jenny a ring. Perhaps they could meet sometime. She had always liked talking to the girl, and she had been very kind.

"Yes I must do that." she decided.

Matthew slowly related the evolution of the Zargon/Earth hybrid to the best of information fed back to him. Jenny had reached the stage where nothing else could shock her. Or so she thought.

There was one mishap that sent shock waves throughout the galaxy. Having produced his perfect specimen, Zargot couldn't wait to put it to the test. A rocket was ready to propel the first 'guinea pig', known as H1, into space and make it land on Zargon. There it would be transferred to a space craft made of zargonite, a metal developed only in that place, and sent back to earth, to the exact point of launch.

But something went wrong. Or was made to go wrong.

"Don't tell me I had anything to do with that." Jenny was not serious.

"You did. With a bit of help I might add."

"What did I do? No wait. I gathered forces and we crashed it in the hopes it would be found, and the earth military would investigate." The words came poring out. "I'm right. I know it."

"Yes, you're right. Only we all know what happened then." Matthew realised the more she heard, the more she was recalling. "Do you want to say it?"

"Let me try. The craft came down, in a field, or part of the desert or something, and a farmer saw it. The army took it away, and -" she paused while the facts sorted themselves into order in her brain. "Oh my god Matthew, they found the hybrid and did an autopsy on it, thinking it was an alien, which of course it half was. Only it had come from here." She finished with a flourish very satisfied.

Matthew gave mock applaud. "Did you remember or were you only guessing." he teased.

"How could I guess that?" Her face then clouded and she spun round.

He knew from her expression, the whole nasty truth had invaded her mind.

He said very gently "Do you want to tell me what you think you know?"

She had gone very pale and was shaking. Suddenly she shook herself, her face full of anger and revenge.

"That monster, took the eggs of my teenage daughter. Then he raped her, he abused her so badly, she was in a mental hospital for the rest of her life here."

Matthew lowered his head is if in memory of the lovely girl. "And when you discovered this, you swore revenge, although it was against your father's wishes."

Jenny was white with fury. "How could I react with love to that thing, how could I forgive. No, I swore it then, and I swear it again. I will not rest through the whole of eternity, until I have repaid the evil he did?" She was on her feet, her fists white to the knuckle.

"You're back." Matthew drew her back to her seat. "One other thing though."

Jenny sat reluctantly and looked towards the heavens. "What?"

"Your daughter was on her final earth visit." He let the words sink in. As recollection hit her the tears ran.

"Marie," she whispered, my beautiful little Marie."

Chapter 19

"Yes. Right. I'll see you next Sunday then. Good bye." Mrs. Randle replaced the receiver and turned to her husband. "There, I told you it would work." Jack eyed his wife suspiciously.

"You're meddling again Gladys. Remember what happened last time. I don't like it, and I don't like it in this house."

"But think of the money" she protested. "Don't try and tell me we don't need it. Have you seen those bills?" She waved at the mantelpiece.

"We've always managed."

"Yes, managed is the word for it. Well I'm sick of managing. I want a bit more. I want that car."

He slammed down the paper. "That's your bloody trouble woman, you always want more. You're never satisfied. Well, you'll get more than you bargain for one of these days."

"You won't laugh when it pays off Jack Randle." She started to set the table for tea.

"But why here?" He wasn't giving in that easily, although he knew deep down she would have her way. "Why don't you hire a hall or something, or do it at other folks' places if they're so keen to contact the departed."

"Oh yes," she flicked the tablecloth to give emphasis to her words, "I'm sure people would be only too pleased with that wouldn't they?" She vigorously smoothed out the creases. "I can just hear it now."

Jack sighed and got up.

"Now where do you think you're going? I'm getting the tea ready."

He paused at the door and said very precisely "I'm going to the lav if it's all the same to you, or do you want to ask them up there if it's alright?" With that he slammed the door behind him.

Gladys Randle was not to be deflated. Everything was going her way, she had had a good response to her advertisement and replied to every letter. One or two were a bit dubious, but her head was in the clouds and she could only see the pound signs lighting up. Her husband had not dampened her enthusiasm, and all she could think of was the coming meeting.

"I can hardly wait for Sunday," she thought to herself as she hummed happily whilst laying the table.

Jimmy passed the door of his daughter's previous bedroom. He stood for a moment with his hand on the knob, then quietly entered and stood before her bed. Kate kept the bed made up in case Jenny ever wanted to stay the night. Jimmy gently caressed the pillow which so many times had held the precious head of his child.

Had Kate seen his expression she would have been more unnerved than when they stood together watching the girl's face distort in her sleep.

Matthew and Jenny were discussing moves. They could converse on an almost equal footing now, instead of teacher and pupil, although Matthew still felt a great responsibility. If anything went wrong now, it might not be so easily remedied the next time.

"I must see Marie. I must let her know." Jenny almost pleaded but the undertone stated this was something she would do anyway. Her husband nodded. "Of course you must." Then after a pause. "You're going tonight?"

"Yes. that's no problem is it?"

"No." Matthew looked serious. "That's fine, but I do feel we should go to Eden at the first opportunity."

"Yes, you're right", she smiled, "tell you what --"

The both chorused in unison "We'll do both." They laughed with a togetherness that made them both realised they needed each other in more ways than one.

As Jenny touched his hand she said, "Can we go to see Marie first?"

"Got a better idea."

"Oh?"

Matthew gave a scheming little smile. "As this is such an important issue, don't you think Marie should be with us on Eden?"

"Oo, crafty, get her to come to us you mean?" Her look told him she could see right through him.

"Makes sense." Then to really lighten the mood he lay back and said "Anyway, how about some tea. Be off to the the kitchen my woman and prepare my food." She almost leapt on him and they hugged with such force her breath nearly left her.

"I love you my archangel Gabriel."

"And I love you my little elfin, or should I call you the good fairy?" He laughed.

She sat back from him, eyed him, then started to run into the house as she said "As long as I don't call you that." She squealed in laughter as he chased her, caught her, and they embraced once more.

"If only things could be like this for ever." She was wistful.

"But it gives us a weapon even HE cannot combat. Love, intense powerful, wonderful love my darling."

Living together had given the newly weds the ideal opportunity of travelling at will. Neither had to make the excuse of going to bed, for whatever reason, they both knew the need to travel when needed, even in daytime. So they decided to waste no more time and visit Eden that very evening.

They settled together on the sofa and were promptly apparently asleep. With one thought they were on Eden. Jenny was surprised to be greeted by Marie then realised the message would have preceded her. The two ideals merged in an emotionally charged moment and Matthew left them to share a few minutes alone, before returning with Graham and other powers.

On Eden, the ideals were neither gender. They were positioned in both sexes on earth to receive as full and open minded learning course as possible. But they remembered earthly relationships past and present, and the love shared therein. This remained with them, but the love was purely spiritual and not physical. The earthly species, were after all, only different to reproduce and carry on the breed, but there were many life forms who were able to self re-produce and did not mate. Since his marriage, Matthew was secretly glad he wasn't one of those, but pushed the impure thought out of his mind immediately. He was on Eden now and must behave accordingly.

Jenny was anxious to meet her father, the Powerful One, but realised one didn't just approach so high a supreme being without preparation. Therefore a meeting was to be held with his next in line, and then she would be given time to cleanse before the audience she so desired.

Immediately under the Powerful One were six ultimate beings, making a hierarchy of seven. The Powerful One never moved from his position, he always reigned supreme. The next six acted in an upward spiral, similar to a kettle of hawks preparing for migration, entering the chimney at the bottom and working their way to the top. Whoever was at the top when divine help was needed, was despatched to that task. The other five moved up, and when the ultimate returned, it would assume the bottom position.

All six often took on the same appearance. In order words, people were shown what they expected to see. One of these six had been sent to Bethlehem to teach the world about love. Another had been sent to close the portal at Mrs. Randle's. And so on. Jenny was one of the six until her Jupiter life trauma, and had to be replaced to keep the seven in tact.

Matthew and Graham were from the seven highly advanced beings immediately below these ultimate ones, and it was Matthew who had been selected to fill Jenny's place, and he knew he would have to stand down when she was fully restored.

The four friends waited anxiously for the ultimate to join them. The area was filled with light which engulfed their ideals until they were conscious of mind alone. Neither could see an image of the other.

The thought came from the ultimate. "Jenny, we hope you are recovered enough to do your double switch. Do you think you can?" This was something only Jenny could do previously although others had tried and failed. It meant she had to switch to a position in thought travel, and switch back almost immediately, and by so doing the enemy rarely knew she had been. But the difficult part was to assimilate everything about her in that split second. If she was spotted, it was so instantaneous, the subject thought it was a trick of the light, or they were overworked. She had used it many times to advantage and it was a valuable tool, if only she could use it now.

Matthew suggested a practice run to somewhere that was unimportant. Then if she couldn't yet do it, the Zargs wouldn't suspect they were being observed. The whole idea of using her talent was that no force knew where the Zargs had positioned. They were certainly well hidden, but it was essential to know what they were planning, if there was to be any chance of overthrowing them. And it needed to be done now.

Jenny decided to try the double switch to her old place of work. There would be nobody there, so if she had a delay in returning, nobody would be any the wiser. The ultimate withdraw and the light faded. The four looked at each other.

"Oh well," Jenny's thought touched them, "Let's see shall we?"

Before they had returned an acknowledgment she had gone, but it was a full five seconds before she returned.

"No good" they all agreed "she would have been seen."

"I nearly was." Jenny related how she had travelled to her old desk, only to notice her ex boss in his office. She had to re-thought quickly to get back.

"But," Graham's thought spread," if George was in physical, he wouldn't have noticed."

Matthew was quick to correct him. "The old fault of assuming has got ideals into more trouble than they need."

Marie joined in. "We assume George was in physical, but if he is a walker, he could have noticed her there."

"I stand corrected. But I think we're nearly there." Graham was hopeful. "It's only time and practice, but the trouble is we don't have the time."

Jenny urged "Let me have another go." There was a slight space vibration.

"Go on then," Marie urged.

"Done it". Jenny was exuberant for two reasons. She was rapidly regaining all her powers, and she could now do what was required of her.

Matthew asked "How much did you absorb?"

Jenny was puzzled. "Quite a bit. George was going through the desk I used to have. I'd left a comb in one of the drawers and he was holding it to him. Strange."

Marie pointed out "Good job he wasn't in that spot when you sent the first time."

As if summoned the ultimate returned. It was decided to use Jenny to double switch to as many deserted earth locations as possible to try and locate Zargot and then eradicate him.

But for now it was time for Jenny to prepare herself for a reunion, in which the presence of the others was not required.

Chapter 20

Gladys Randle was hardly able to contain herself. It was Sunday, and this afternoon she would be able to once again let herself go at what she did best. That was her opinion.

"I must make sure I get the money first," she fussed over the room, drew the curtains, made sure the candles were all in exactly the right place and slowly closed the door as if a draught would disturb something.

Jack still wasn't happy with it, and he told her so. He wanted to put his feet up, watch a film and nod off if he felt so inclined. Instead, what had he got to look forward to. A load of folks with more money than sense, and him stuck behind a curtain doing his wife's bidding.

"It's fraud" he once told her. "I'm doing the things they think are coming from the other side."

"That's where you are wrong,"she had scolded. "I've never heard of such a thing. You only help to set the scene, the rest is then up to me."

After lunch, Gladys quickly cleared away and changed into her 'mystic smock'.

"How many idiots can we expect?" Jack didn't mind voicing his views to the very last.

"I told you Jack. I had ten replies, but I think only eight may come. I've given them until 2.30pm." She emphasized the time in that way.

Jack grunted. "Half past two to most people." After a moment he looked at his watch and said "I'll be glad when it's over."

A knock at the door sent Gladys scurrying to answer it. She ushered in a middle aged husband and wife, shortly followed by two teenage girls who had only come as a dare. All were seated in the lounge until everyone was present.

"Only a couple of minutes," Gladys assured them, then we will start. "Ah, there's somebody else now." An elderly lady who wanted to be reunited with her cat joined the party.

"Usual type." Gladys thought as she collected the payments. the next customer was a total surprise, and not one who had answered the advert. It was George, her boss.

At 2.30pm prompt, the assorted gathering was led into the dining room and seated at the table. The room appeared to be in total darkness, thanks to the heavy curtains which were drawn across the window but gradually, as their eyes became accustomed to the gloom, they all noticed tiny candles spread around the outside.

When they were all seated, Gladys lit a spicy scented candle in the centre of the table and requested they all join hands. The girls started to giggle, partly from nerves wishing they had never come.

"Ladies." Mrs. Randle's voice took on a hollow ghostly tone, well rehearsed. "We must control ourselves. There will be forces here today which must not be taken lightly. If you cannot accept this, please leave now." "But you won't get your money back." she thought.

The two girls settled down with mumbled apologies, and kicked each other under the table.

The candle smoke was a little heady and making a few eyes water. Just right. Mrs. Randle began.

She went through the preliminaries of calling her guide and asking if he had any messages. Jack set the tape going. An eerie meowing floated across the room.

"It's Timmy. It's my little Timmy." the old lady cried. "Are you alright my little one?"

Mrs. Randle started to sway from side to side and gave the poor dear a message from her beloved Timmy. Jack stifled a sneeze and thought "I wish she wouldn't use those smelly things."

A few moments pause. The girls were thinking it wasn't as bad as they thought, and at least they had won the bet. They were still holding hands when one of them felt a pressure on her knee. She quickly looked around, peering through the smoke haze. All hands were still joined. She was about to speak when Mrs. Randle let out a cry. "I have a message for somebody here today. His name begins with the letter, J or could it be G?"

"I'm George." Cue for Jack to press another control. Very soft organ music floated out, barely audible at first, but then almost in tune to the medium's voice.

"I need you George, I am your brother." She remembered him taking time from work to go to the funeral a few months ago. Lucky that, seeing as he had turned up without an appointment. But she was happy to take his money and give him a good run for it.

She expected George to speak but he was silent. Why was he here if he didn't want to make contact?

The next moment there was a terrific downdraught, blowing out all the candles and leaving the room in total blackness. The females all screamed, and even the men felt the hair rise on their necks. Instinctively they tried to break hands but were held in a powerful force which seemed to be pulling them into the centre of the table. Jack gingerly peered out from behind his curtain but was immediately thrust back and held there.

An eerie column of green light fell onto the group and a dank chill engulfed them. The image of a creature formed in the mist. A mixture of animal and human, it rose until its head was at the ceiling, its body disappearing into the table. Mrs. Randle was actually in a trance her eyes closed. The girls tried to scream but it choked in their throats. The others could only look on in horror as the entity seemed to envelope them one by one. Just as quickly it disappeared and the candles re-lit by themselves. But instead of being spaced around the room they were all on the floor by the window curtain. It only took seconds for the material to ignite, the flames licking as if trying to feed a hunger.

Panic set in. The middle aged couple fled from the house immediately. The girls were sobbing and one was being physically sick as her friend dragged her out side. The old lady stayed at the table motionless, the shock had killed her. Mrs. Randle was just coming out of her trance as her husband rushed from his hiding place with the intention of pulling her to safety before he tried to fight the fire which had now taken hold. On realising he would stand no chance, he got his wife outside and yelled to a neighbour to call the fire brigade. A few people were gathering, wondering what was going on. The four members of the meeting were comforting each other and paying little heed to the safety of their hosts. Only one person could not be accounted for. Nobody saw George leave, and when the fire officers searched the remains of the room, only the badly charred body of the old lady, now reunited with her Timmy, was found. It was assumed he had made his escape through the window, but that theory was soon squashed. Even with the damage, the window frames were in the closed position. Had he broken the glass and if so why? It would have been easier to have made his escape with the others, and it would have been friendly to see that the others were all right and accounted for. But it seemed that George had simply disappeared.

Jimmy sat in his armchair alone in his thoughts. Kate could be heard washing up and muttering to herself as she cleared the kitchen.

"Have you put the telly on yet?" she called out.

"Um, no, doing it now." He reached over, switched on the set, and sat back not watching the screen, his mind engulfed in his daughter. How he missed her. She'd only been gone a couple of weeks but he felt a void as if she had been taken from him for good. There was no reason for such a reaction. He'd always loved her dearly, left her to her own quiet little ways but been there if she had ever needed him, which sadly, she hadn't. He thought the ache would disappear after a few days, but it was steadily getting worse. He didn't want to talk to Kate about it in case it upset her.

"It was a big enough wrench for her anyway," he mused as she joined him to watch one of the soaps.

"You're looking tired Jim, "she peered at him, "been overdoing it at work again I expect."

"Probably." was all he would say.

Chapter 21

Mrs. and Mrs. Gavrielle jnr. were back in their home. There was no need to remain on Eden and leave their light lines exposed, also Jenny could just as easily double switch from any location. As there was no time to loose, it had been agreed that Graham would also return to physical and drive over to sit with Matthew while Jenny started her enormous task. Together they would stay near her form to protect her return. They could each leave their own forms but return quickly if the need arose.

"This is some mammoth undertaking." Jenny was preparing to depart for the first time.

"I know my love, but you are the only one who can do it." Matthew held her hand. "I will be here for you, and so will Graham, and of course Marie's ideal will be at hand."

Jenny's eyes narrowed. "Do you know something?"

"What's that?"

"He, Zargot, thinks I won't destroy his hybrids."

Matthew looked bemused. "Why shouldn't you? Oh wait a minute, because one or some could be-- "

"Go on say it," her eyes flashed "they could be my offspring. If Marie's eggs were used, some of the creatures could be my grandchildren."

"And that wouldn't make you hesitate?"

"That's why he did it. He though he would always hold a trump card. Well, he didn't reckon with me." She drew in her breath. "I would rather release the poor things from those tombs in which they are forced to exist."

She had always referred to the hybrids as being in Zargot's tombs. The Z -Tombies, which was converted in earthly terms to Zombies - the living dead.

"Here's Graham" Matthew had heard the car and was on his feet making his way to the door.

"Thanks for coming straight over Graham, "Jenny greeted him with a kiss.

"Least I could do. Only wish we could do it with you."

"Don't worry, it's enough you're here."

The all settled on the sofa, Jenny in the centre, held hands, and closed their eyes.

It was decided to eliminate the smaller deserts first, and then concentrate on the larger ones methodically. It was absolutely vital that Jenny remain undetected until the operation was complete, however long it would take.

After many double switches, Jenny said "I think I will take a short break, it's taxing me more than I thought it would." So saying, she closed her eyes and rested.

"Did you hear something?" Matthew's acute hearing tuned into a sound from outside.

"Such as?" Graham immediately picked up his friend's warning tone. They each went to a window but darkness had fallen and neither could see anything. They noticed Jenny had fallen asleep and decided to leave her for a moment while they went outside. At the door Matthew halted suddenly.

"I must be slipping," he held up his hand to stop Graham in his tracks,"quick get back to Jenny, we'll use walk mode."

Jenny was still fast asleep. "Must have taken it out of her." Graham said.

Matthew sat down and 'walked' his ideal outside to see if he could trace the source of the sound which had disturbed him. Only the whisperings of the nocturnal creatures reached him. There was nothing physical, no wandering ideals, only the stirring of the grass in the night breeze. He returned to his body.

"She's still asleep then?" he asked Graham.

"It may be nothing, "the doubt was enough to stir Matthew's instincts.

"WHAT?" he almost shouted.

Graham looked at Jenny then back at Matthew. "She seems too still."

Matthew was at her side in a flash. "What were we thinking of? We shouldn't have let her sleep." Both tried desperately to wake her but to no avail.

"Stay here." Matthew ordered "I'm going to speed mode. And whatever you do, DO NOT SLEEP."

Matthews's body appeared reposed at the side of his wife's, while Graham sat on full alert, waiting.

Jenny had only drifted momentarily, but being caught off guard had been swept up in a spiral of green light which moved across the countryside light a tornado, touching down where it chose.

"An open portal" the horror swept through her ideal as she realised she could be pulled at force to the top opening, her light line severed, hence her return to her body halted.

Depending on the entity opening a portal, the format could vary. A lesser fiend could only leave the opening in it's original position making it easier to trace, but moving father up the iniquitous ladder, a portal could be made to sway or travel, leaving it's opening of origin undetected. In some case never to be used again once the evil force had been unleashed. Here lay the danger with the meddlers, and dabblers such as Mrs. Randle, who had now exposed the earth to an army of corrupt forces summoned by the arch demon himself, Zargot.

Jenny's energy was drained by her double switches and she wished she had paced herself a little more, but the task was so urgent she had pressed on with one thought urging her. The destruction of Zargot. As she was twisted and flung within the vortex, she felt her ideal being sucked higher and higher. She tried to blot the green film with a powerful direct hit of heavenly blue light. It held her for an instant, but slowly she was being drawn further up. If it got her to the top, that would be the end of her last earth life. One final hope reached her.

"My Father." her whole ideal screamed for him. But the answer was not that simple. He could not send the forces to close the portal, while she was still inside. She would have to be pulled out first.

A message was immediately transferred to all highly experienced ideals to hold and protect the light line, whilst the portal closers stood by in readiness. Such was the operation, that two from the ultimate six were despatched, one to help hold, and one to oversee the close.

Although the evil entity was certainly a powerful one, it was no match for such a combined force that was aimed at it. Very slowly, Jenny was lowered until she escaped from the bottom of the green light funnel. The closing group moved forward and exorcized the area from the ungodly invaders.

Jenny opened her eyes, looked from Matthew to Graham and then around the room.

"It's alright," Matthew assured her, "you're back."

"Where did I slip up?" She could have sobbed with weakness and frustration, but her inner fight would not allow it.

"You didn't, we did. We shouldn't have let you nod off." Matthew smiled gently.

"Do you know what?" She turned to Graham. "I don't know about ideal needs, but my physical is gasping for a cup of tea."

"That's my girl." Matthew hugged her. Then turning to Graham he said, "You know where everything is don't you?"

"Well, no," was the reply," but I think I'm about to find out." This banter had lightened the mood for a moment, but when Graham had returned with the tea, they all sat to discuss the implications of the life threatening experience Jenny had just endured.

The police had interviewed the Randles following the death of the old lady in the fire. Gladys had tried to cover up as much as she could, but the two teenagers were so terrified they had related the whole incident in detail. A priest had been called in to rid the building of anything that may be still lurking, before it was closed off for safety reasons. It looked as though Gladys would face a charge of murder, or manslaughter, which, added to the fact of the house being gutted, and Jack having gone to their son's to get over the ordeal, left her almost alone. Her sister, who also lived in the village, but with whom she had never really got on, took her in on a temporary basis simply to give her a roof over her head while the police enquiries continued.

She had not been to work, and it looked unlikely that she would return to her job as she couldn't face George after such a nightmare. Had she only known? The police went to interview him as one of the guests at the meeting, but he had a perfect alibi and knew nothing of the event. He was concerned for Mrs. Randle and asked how she was. The general opinion was that Mrs. R. had imagined he was there, or somebody like him had attended the séance. As she was the only one who knew him, nobody could confirm his identity. The others said there was a man on his own, but paid little heed to him, all being intent on their own reasons for being there combined with the smoky atmosphere and barely any light. The final terror had taken pride of place in everyone's mind and although everyone tried to describe him, the end product was such a mixture, it was hardly plausible.

Zargot was very pleased with himself. He was gathering together all the forces he could muster. Some were only too pleased to be with him, than against him, but if they thought this action would curry favour, they should have known better. This demon used ideals, bodily forms, entities, in fact anything he could control at the time, but having served its purpose he would then dispose of it with such sadistic pleasure, as to make the most hardened veteran force shudder.

Unlike the Powerful One on Eden who never left his position as head of the spiral, Zargot would, when the need arose, give his full attention to the matter in hand, whether it be on earth, another planet or asteroid, or any area in which he could plant his evil seeds.

He was certain he would be undetected this time until he was ready to strike. His sentinels were keeping track of the Powerful One's daughter and taking every opportunity to weaken her newly found strength. Being who he was, he had an additional weapon at his command which surpassed anything used by lesser evils who would take possession of a particular person or place until exorcised. Zargot could easily possess a body for a short time, taking on whatever appearance he wished. He would then transfer to another unsuspecting person, thus confusing those trying to track him.

Some were easier to take over than others, usual weak willed mortals, but especially those who left their doors open for him to walk in. The silly fools who played with ouija boards were ideal. He had had a lot of fun with ouija boards. But Mrs. Randle's séance was just too easy. Although he didn't need the portal for his own use, he was not going to let such a chance go by. He was playing on the fact that the' holy ones', as he sarcastically referred to them, having once closed the portal would leave the area unguarded, not expecting it to be re-opened.

Had they only be prepared for this happening, the forces on Eden would have had him in their grasp.

Chapter 22

The forces on Eden were getting rather concerned, to say nothing of Jenny's feeling of failure. Zargot had been flitting from one host to another so rapidly, it was some task to keep up with him. It was obvious where he had been, but where he was going to appear next was the problem.

He had toyed with the idea of using Jimmy to get to Jenny, but didn't find the character to his liking. The impure thoughts about the man's daughter he had so carefully placed were immediately rejected with such revulsion, he moved away for pastures new.

George had provided the perfect carrier. Having been to a friend's stag night on the Saturday night, he and a few of his mates had crashed out at one of the single lad's homes in the next village and slept off the effects of the strong beverage for most of Sunday. Zargot had taken over George as he slept, driven his car to the séance, and got him out of the house before the fire started. He had then returned him to his sleeping position, left his body, and discarded him with no knowledge of his movements. Thus he moved around the area leaving little or no trace.

After about three months of this cat and mouse game, in which Zargot was the cat, playing with its prey until ready to pounce for the kill, Matthew and Jenny were watching television and generally discussing space communication.

"Isn't it funny?" Jenny was saying, "There are these organisations who do nothing but search for extra terrestrial life or messages. This man, "she nodded towards the television," says that we aren't receiving and messages because there probably is no-one out there."

Matthew laughed. "We could tell him a thing or two, couldn't we?"

"Hang on, "Jenny listened for a moment, "perhaps we are receiving messages but in a form we don't understand, or perhaps the aliens don't want to communicate."

"What you are saying, "Matthew sat back and crossed his legs "is that the truth isn't out there, it's down here, and has been all along.

They are so busy with their dishes trying to look further and further, when all the time, what they are seeking is right here under their dirty little noses."

"THAT'S IT." Jenny was on her feet switching off the set. "My archangel Gabriel, you are wonderful." She hugged and kissed her husband, and while he was enjoying seeing her so vibrant, he was still wondering what he had said to cause such a reaction.

"Don't you see?" Her eyes were bright with enthusiasm at having solved the problem which had eluded them for so long.

"Calm down, and tell me slowly."

He sat her down next to him and she composed her thoughts.

"I know where we've been going wrong, and I think I know how to beat Zargot."

Matthew looked relieved but hesitant. "Go on."

"Well, it was when you said the truth was under their noses. You see, I've been double switching all over the earth, searching the plains, the deserts, oh you name it. I've searched it. And what did I find?"

"Nothing." Matthew agreed wishing she would get to the point.

"If he is here to attack me, where will he be? Where will his evil be directed?"

"At you of course." It was so clear to Matthew, now it had been put on a plate before him. "Instead of you searching for him, we should have realised he would be close. He can muster his forces from any point; he doesn't have to be there with them."

"You won't like the next bit."

Matthew knew he wouldn't. "I won't?"

"I will have to draw him in."

"Jenny no, you can't do that."

"Why not. It's time he was flushed out. Think how strong I am now. While he has been playing the waiting game, my power has not been drained, it has increased. In fact, I would guess it's just about fully restored."

Matthew looked away. "I don't like it. It's too dangerous."

"Oh don't worry, we'll get help."

"Well, that's a relief anyway," he didn't sound convinced. "I think."

Jenny smiled at him. "Could we get Graham in on this? I want you two to work together."

"Sure. Shall I call him straight away?"

"Might as well. Why waste time."

Graham was there in half an hour and was soon listening, overawed at this woman's courage. When she was sure she had their total concentration, she sat opposite them and began.

"Unlike my father, the Powerful One who never leaves his post unguarded, Zargot loves to travel and spread as much evil as he can. Now, he usually takes one of his upper spiral with him, he's even been know to take two or three when the odds were stacked against him. He spreads them out in his image so the poor creatures in his power think it is him. "

The two men were drinking in her every word in silence.

"I don't need to remind you that, unlike our upper spiral, which works in an orderly fashion, utter unison and no questions asked, the evil ones are always struggling for top position, fighting amongst themselves, especially when boss man is not there to keep them in order."

Matthew nudged Graham. "I think I'm beginning to see what she's driving at."

Jenny smiled. "If I can draw Zargot to me, complete with entourage, and don't forget I have a score to settle, it will leave his base poorly protected, and his spiral weak. This is where you come in."

Graham shifted uneasily. "It sounds very dangerous Jen. I don't like the thought of you fighting him and his little satellites alone."

Matthew cut in "I've said that" but Jenny held up her hand to stop him.

"Don't you think what I'm asking you to do is equally perilous?"

They looked at each other, now thinking it could work. It had got to work.

Jenny still held the floor. "I'm going now to meet with my father. I want one of our ultimates to help you. That should be all the power you will need."

"And you?" Matthew said quietly, "What help are you requesting?"

Jenny very slowly sat down and simply said "I wasn't the only mother."

Zargot was looking for another host. Someone who could get close to Jenny in the earthly form without her suspecting it. But it would have to be somebody not already high in power, some innocent little soul who could be manipulated and controlled to carry out his deadly deed for him. He had wasted enough time and was tired of the chase. It was time for the kill.

Jenny returned from her thought switch to Eden. "It's all settled, although my father has warned me that vengeance is not mine to take. He also reminded me that you are still in the upper spiral Matthew, until my re-instating and you will lead the attack on Zargon. He cannot release another ultimate to you in case one should be required to assist me and he will not jeopardise the safety of our own spiral by despatching too many."

"When do we go?" Graham was a little apprehensive.

"I'm afraid, "Jenny looked from one to the other "it's right now."

"Not much time to prepare," Matthew said.

"The Schynings are going to help you, and I have my own resources, before you both ask again."

Jenny indicated for the men to get up.

"You mean we can't go from here?" Graham was prepared to get settled on the sofa.

"Think about it." Matthew was already looking for his jacket. "If Zargot should come here and notice we are in some sort of travel mode--" he let his voice trail off.

"Go as far as you can," Jenny ordered "get your light lines as great a distance from here, just in case. But don't tell me where. I don't want the thought."

"Give us an hour then." Matthew had gathered up some belongings and was steering Graham towards the door. They both kissed her but leaving her was the hardest thing for them. Leaving her to the evil power which was about to take her in its grasp.

Mrs. Randle was nearing a breakdown. She couldn't stop crying, and was haunted by the events of the séance. "I'm possessed, I'm possessed,"she would cry.

"She will be in a minute," her sister would mutter, "and it won't be by the other side, it will be from my fist."

Jack had visited, but still felt he couldn't stay in her presence a moment longer than was necessary. "You're a wicked woman" was all he could say. As he left he told the sister "I warned her, I knew she'd come unstuck."

Zargot hovered. Now here was a likely specimen. Maybe he could use the wretch, besides; it had been very generous of her to open the portal. Yes, it was time she had what she had wanted for so long, a brush with the other side. Tomorrow he would visit her again.

Matthew and Graham had travelled for nearly an hour, when they stopped the car at a travel lodge. Booking into a room as two business men they soon settled down to the task before them.

"We mustn't strike before Jenny is ready," Matthew said as they left their physical forms, If we do, he will be pulled back to Zargon and we need him separated from as many of his most powerful as possible."

They confirmed the Schynings were ready along, with many others only too willing to help crush the deadly beings, even for a limited time.

Graham asked "How will we know?"

"We'll be told." was the reply.

Jenny was alone. She sent out various messages knowing they would be intercepted, and waited. Marie was at a safe distance heading an almighty band of ideals, some who had been victims of the terrible mutilations, some who had been parents, but all with a score to settle.

Suddenly there was a knock at the door. "Oh no, not now." Jenny was somewhat cautious. The house was in its own walled grounds with a long gravel drive. Not the sort of place you happened to be passing. Quickly she gathered her wits, went into a double switch to the front door, and with a mixture of relief and surprise saw her mother standing there.

"Mum, what are you doing here?" she opened the door to admit her.

"Well, that's a nice welcome I must say." she put one foot in the door but was stopped immediately.

"Just one moment." Jenny's hand held her back. "How did you get here?"

"Oh Jenny, I had a lift, you're poor dad's ill and---"

"Why didn't you ring?" She realised this was no human, this was an image of what she was supposed to see and trust. But Jenny knew this was what she had been anticipating for so long.

The form in front of her melted into a being, not hideous but reeking of everything evil. Behind it were two other forms so transparent she could hardly make them out, but she could feel their unearthly presence. She knew if this was to work, she could not crumble before them but must take a stand until her back up arrived. The images flooded her mind of all the misformed creatures crying in torment after the indignities they had been subjected to by this entity before her. She stood tall rising above it, surveying the trio with such contempt.

"So. You thought you would outwit me did you?" she cleared her mind of all else lest they should pick up on her tactics.

Zargot brought the two flankers closer to him for a combined attack. She rose from her body until she was above the house, the foe following her every move, their forces locked ready for the other to release the hold. Immediately, Marie and her army were behind her releasing the hatred of their pent up emotions. Jenny felt her strength growing. She pointed at him and felt his unseen grasp wrap itself around her arm. Unrelenting, she held the force matching its power with a greater one. They twisted in the air, the whole sky electric with the two almighty powers locked in fierce battle.

Marie knew Jenny was capable of overcoming Zargot alone, so her group set about splitting away the two supporters. If anyone has never seen a group of mothers let loose on someone who, at some time abused their little babies, they would do well to heed what followed, for it would be a deterrent to would be rapists, attackers and child abusers everywhere. Had the entities been human, nothing over the size of a square inch would have remained.

They split the almost see through forms, pulling, stretching, and mutilating.

Jenny knew she had him now. Seeing what was going on around her, she was fuelled by the torment these fiends were enduring. They existed in mind like her race on Eden, but she was aware that torture of the mind could be as powerful and longer lasting than any physical injuries they could have endured.

The message had gone out to Matthew and all combined forces rushed Zargon heading for the high place. As suspected the four left in the higher spiral were each trying to assume command and were not prepared for the bombardment which followed. Using the lightning power of the Schynings, Matthew followed with his troupe, locked themselves into mental combat with two of the evil ultimates, followed immediately by Graham and party taking the remainder.

It was all over very quickly, but not before one had sent a message down to the lower beings who transmitted it to Zargot, reaching him as Jenny was crushing his force, ready to despatch it. The tattered trio departed as one, leaving the night air calm.

Jenny exchanged thoughts with Marie and her angels as they would always be known. Emotions were very high as they thanked Jenny for the chance to get just a little even, although they all knew, nothing would ever wipe their grief completely. Equally she was grateful for the support and she watched as they helped each other away. She and Marie shared a very precious moment together before Jenny regained her body, still at the front door, but slumped on the step.

Chapter 23

The Powerful One had extended Matthew's stay on earth following his success in restoring Jenny to her former power. It was felt that, although Zargot had been defeated for now, he wouldn't be long trying to take revenge for loosing face for the second time. This was reward indeed and Matthew phoned Jenny from the travel lodge to tell her what he felt she would already know, but couldn't resist revelling in the earthly husband/wife relationship.

"We'll be home soon," he blew a kiss down the receiver.

"I'll be fine if you want to come in the morning. I can always meet you in thought or speed."

"No, we can't wait to get back. I've said Graham can stay, that's alright isn't it. Can you make a bed up?

"Consider it done." She blew a kiss back.

"Oh hang on," Matthew was laughing, "you should see this man, he's just popped his head out of the bathroom to say he'll sleep on the floor."

"See you in an hour then." Jenny replaced the receiver and made her way upstairs to get the spare bed ready.

The two men were discussing the events on the way home. "The old boy will be licking his wounds a bit now." Graham felt the weight lifted from them and was relaxing already.

"Yes, but the scraps of evil left in position to fester will soon be nurtured, and he could return more vengeful than ever."

They drove into the night watching the speeding lights in the heavens.

"Not long now, "Matthew was eager to hold his wife in his physical arms as soon as possible. They were approaching a bend when Graham shouted "Look out, that old man in the road!" Matthew swerved to miss him, he went straight through him, swerved across the verge and hit a tree.

Marie was called to assist a double transition, but when she arrived and saw her two friends hovering above the car, she crumbled. They should have been experienced enough to know the procedure, but Matthew could only think of Jenny waiting for his physical to return and was distraught. Graham suggested visiting her and explaining first hand, but she would be awake, so it wouldn't be easy.

"He didn't take long getting even." Matthew was angry with himself. He should have kept up his guard every second of the way.

"I think the task will be done for you," Marie indicated to the police car at the scene. A message was already being sent to another vehicle to break the news to the bereaved.

"Should we go to her?" Graham said in thought.

"I don't know if I can bear to see her upset, after all she's done tonight." But Marie faced them both. "Let's all go. She will try to reach us in thought immediately she hears."

"Of course." Matthew should have worked that out but it had been quite a night.

Jenny had assured the policewoman she would be alright on her own. It had been suggested they fetch Kate and Jimmy over to stay with her, but she insisted against it. She did ask if they would ring Matthew's parents in Spain for her, she couldn't manage that. The Gavrielle seniors demanded in a kindly way, to speak to her, so she had a few brief words and they arranged to get the first flight home in the morning.

She spent the rest of the night with her departed husband and her two friends, satisfied at the outcome of the temporary crushing of Zargot, but shattered by the immediate retaliation.

Matthew's parents would have liked their son to have his own funeral, but Jenny insisted on a joint one.

"They were together in life, and they will be together in death" she had said but thought "more than you know." Her wreath was a heart of white flowers, trimmed with blue ribbon and the card read "Our White Noise Will Always Be Heavenly Blue."

Everyone was very supportive for a while, as people are, but then life goes on and people drift away, often coping with their own tribulations. Her parents in law wanted her to go to Spain with them, but she politely refused, agreeing to stay on in their home. Although she could see Matthew every time she travelled, there was a physical longing for him, and an unfulfilled deep rooted ache that was almost controlling her waking life.

Christmas was approaching, although she hadn't got the heart for it. To please her parents, she agreed to see the doctor before the season got under way.

"You've been proper peaky my girl." Her mother would cluck like an old hen. "I know you've been through a lot, but perhaps he can give you a tonic."

No amount of tonic could have cured Jenny's condition. She was pregnant.

As if sent by messenger, the thought came at night. Graham has one more life, but it will be a short one. "If he is repositioned in my baby, I will loose him straight away." After what had happened to Marie in one of her previous lives, surely this would be harsh. She needed this child of her husband to act as a reminder of their too short a marriage. There was only one way to find out.

She thought travelled to Eden and almost demanded to have audience with her father. Kindly but firmly she was reminded that no-one, even she demanded of him. A request would be granted, but she could not make or bend the rules. Graham's re-position had not yet been decided and she felt this rather unfair after her fight with Zargot. Surely this could be arranged.

Her father had replied in his peaceful calm way." My child, you will always be fighting the forces of evil, as they fight us. You went into battle with revenge uppermost in your thoughts, and not the power of love as is my teaching. You have to learn you cannot bargain your way. You fought and you won, for now. You do not try to claim your own reward. It is reward enough that you overcame the power. That should be your satisfaction."

She had returned like a naughty child, well and truly put in its place. There was no alternative, but to wait and hope.

The baby boy was born in early June. There was no doubt as to the name chosen for him. "Gabriel." Jenny announced to a surprised Kate.

"What sort of name is that?" Then rocking him in her arms added, "Well I might have known you'd stick with something biblical, after his father." She saw her daughter's face pucker and said hastily "Oh I'm sorry, it's still early days."

Jenny composed herself. "No, no Mum it's alright. We must talk about him, mention his name. He's not forgotten, and never will be." She took Gabriel back and nursed him, deep in thought. He wasn't Graham. She should have known he wouldn't be, but the consolation was that he would not be snatched from her, so maybe there was wisdom in her father's methods. There usually was, although it was often hard to see it at the time.

"He's making sure I learn everything the hard way." she smiled to herself.

Gabriel was two months old and looking just like his mother. Kate idolised him and Jimmy would sit with him on his knee contentedly telling him things only for lad's ears. This amused the ladies. Kate would often quietly beckon to Jenny and say "You've got to come and see this," and the two would peer unseen at the pair engrossed in their own little world. Jenny was now glad Graham had not been born into this precious little life for she could not bear the thought of parting with another physical form just yet.

There was a village fete in Shipton and Kate had talked Jenny into staying overnight on the Saturday and then going home on the Sunday. This seemed good sense and gave the doting grandparents extra chance to drool over Gabriel. Jenny had a carry cot for the baby and was to sleep in her old room, still the same as when she lived there.

Gabriel was the centre of attention all afternoon, with all the females wanting to give him a love. He lapped it up and there were many jokes about how many hearts he would break before he was much older. The happy little family went back to the cottage and Jenny gave her son his feed for which he was more than ready. Kate wanted to burp him, which his mum was more than happy for her to do.

"How about changing him while, you're at it?" Jenny laughed as she sterilised his bottle.

"I've done it before and I expect I shall do it again." Kate was enjoying being useful.

"I should have expected that." Jenny thought as she finished in the kitchen, joined her mother and lifted Gabriel into her arms.

"Who's a nice sweet smelling little boy now?" and she leaned him towards her mum and dad for them to kiss him. Taking him up the stairs, she couldn't help but recap over the last two years. Went out with Matthew at eighteen. Married him at nineteen. Mother at twenty. "I shouldn't think there will be anything earth shattering next year, but perhaps I'll have my hands full with you little man." Laying him in his cot, she kissed his forehead and whispered, "Goodnight my archangel Gabriel." The reply was never heard.

Matthew, Graham and Marie all looked at the scene.

"Goodnight my little elfin," Matthew still felt the emotion of never having held his son.

"Don't worry,"Marie thought to him, "Jenny's helping tonight, make the most of that."

"When are you bringing him down?" Kate asked half asleep.

"Oh at the end of this programme, there's only a few more minutes." Jenny yawned. "He'll be ready for his next feed."

"I'll get it, you fetch him," her mother said as the credits went up.

"Where's my little man?" Jenny called softly as she opened the door. Gabriel lay still in his cot. Jenny rushed over and lifted him. His lifeless body lay in her arms as she almost fell down the stairs tears streaming down her face.

"He's dead, he shouldn't be dead, he's not Graham." Her mother distraught herself didn't take in the impact of what was being said. She merely thought Jenny was being hysterical.

Marie and Graham watched as Matthew, cradled his son's ideal. He looked up. "I've done this many times while he was in body, but now I will look after him for Jenny."

The tiny ideal had completed it's final earth life and could now progress to it's destiny but there would always be a bond between it and these three who were waiting to take it over and it's earthly mother who could only hold it in it's ideal form.

Chapter 24

And so, as Kate watched Jenny resting on the lounger under the trees in the cottage garden, she again wondered how this girl would cope with the tragedies that had filled the last year. To marry and loose her husband and friend was more than enough, but little Gabriel. Her eyes brimmed with tears but she quickly wiped them on her apron.

"I've got to be strong for her. She's going to need me." The tears still came.

She dabbed her face under the cold tap and composed herself.

"I'll go and sit with her for a while," she said aloud as she made her way to where her daughter lay.

She appeared to be still asleep and Kate wondered whether to leave her in peace and let her have the rest she so badly needed, but something made her finish her steps until she was looking down at the face she had seen distorted so many times.

The eyes were open, staring. The mouth ajar. Jenny was dead. Kate's instinct was to run for help but she stopped. Sobbing she cradled her baby kissing her frantically. She stayed there for several moments, then slowly went into the house and rang for her doctor to come out. Jimmy seemed to be there in a second, but time plays funny tricks with people in distress.

Doctor James confirmed the death, although gently told the parents a post mortem would be needed to identify the cause.

An earthly onlooker would have seen two desperately sad parents trying in vain to comfort each other after an unbelievably tragic chapter in anyone's life.

An ideal would have seen Jenny, after a period of re-adjustment, take her rightful place in the upper spiral of the Powerful One who reigns supreme. Matthew joined Graham in the lower spiral along with Marie.

As the Powerful One surveyed the earth, there was much at peace, but the evil left there was incubating and there was still unrest in certain areas.

The carefully hidden hybrids had not been traced this time, but they were there, waiting.

Waiting for Zargot's revenge.

THE END

About the Author

Tabbie Browne grew up in the Cotswolds in central England which is where she gets the inspiration for her novels. Her father had very strong spiritual beliefs and she feels he guides her but always with a warning to stay in control of your own mind.

Her earliest recollection of writing was at primary school and it has seemed to play a part at significant times during her life. She thinks it is only when we are forced to take step back and unclutter our minds for a while we realise our potential. This point was proved when she slipped a disc, and being very immobile had to write in pencil as the ink would not flow upwards! At this time she wrote many comical poems which, when able again, performed to many audiences. Comedy is very difficult but you know if you are a success with a live audience.

In 1991 as a collector of novelty salt and pepper shakers, she realised there was no book in the UK devoted entirely to the subject. So she wrote one. Which meant she achieved the fact that it was the first of its kind in the country and it sold well to like collectors not only in the UK but in the USA.

Another large upheaval came when she was diagnosed with breast cancer, and due to the extreme energy draining, found it difficult to work for an employer. So she took a freelance journalist course and was pleased to have articles accepted, her main joy being the piece about her father and his life in the village. Again the inspiration area.

But the novels were eating away inside and drawing on her experience at stamp and coin fairs she wrote *'A Fair Collection'* which she serialised in the magazine 'Squirrels' for people who hoard things.

When she wrote *'White Noise Is Heavenly Blue'* and its sequel *'The Spiral'* she sat at the keyboard and the titles just came to her, as did the content of the books. There is no way she could write the plot first as she never knew what was coming next, almost as if somebody was dictating, and for that reason she could never change anything.

Loves:
Animals,
Also performing in live theatre and working as a tv supporting artiste.

Hates:
Bad manners,
Insincere people.

Printed in Great Britain
by Amazon